She'd come to take back what he'd stolen from her.

She *was* a mother and, while she might not have the first idea how to be one, she certainly knew how to fight and so she'd fight for her son.

Clinging to that thought, Solace forced away the fear and steeled herself as she stared straight back into Galen's burning blue eyes.

"Yes," she said coldly. "I took some pictures. Of you and I."

His hands on her wrists tightened. "Why?"

She swallowed, her mouth dry, her heartbeat like a drum in her head. But when she spoke, her voice was steady. "To blackmail you with, of course."

There was no point pretending anymore, and in a way, it was a relief that finally the moment was here. She'd come a long way in six months and her plan had ended up being wildly successful, and soon the awful mistake she'd made would be fixed.

The look on Galen's face was terrible. "Blackmail me for what? Money? Power?"

"No." Solace held tight to her own rage. The rage that had dragged her out of that pit and put her feet on the path that had led here. "I couldn't care less about money or power. What I want, Galen Kouros, is my son."

Three Ruthless Kings

Romance cannot be ruled...

At university, royal friends Galen Kouros, Khalil ibn Amir Al-Nazari and Augustine Solari were known as the wicked princes, causing mayhem wherever they went! Now, they're the three ruthless kings, each responsible for a whole nation, wielding more power than many could comprehend.

But even from their gilded thrones, there is one thing these kings are about to learn they cannot control...

Solace Ashworth is back and there's one thing she wants from Galen...their son! Read on in:

Wed for Their Royal Heir

Look out for Khalil's story:

Khalil hasn't forgotten the contract Sidonie Sullivan signed years ago. Now he's about to make her his queen!

And discover Augustine's story:

Rumors abound that Winifred Fox is carrying playboy King Augustine's baby...

Both coming soon!

Jackie Ashenden

—

WED FOR THEIR
ROYAL HEIR

HARLEQUIN
PRESENTS

HARLEQUIN®
PRESENTS™

ISBN-13: 978-1-335-58421-2

Wed for Their Royal Heir

Copyright © 2023 by Jackie Ashenden

Harlequin Enterprises ULC
22 Adelaide St. West, 41st Floor
Toronto, Ontario M5H 4E3, Canada
www.Harlequin.com

Printed in U.S.A.

Jackie Ashenden writes dark, emotional stories with alpha heroes who've just gotten the world to their liking only to have it blown apart by their kick-ass heroines. She lives in Auckland, New Zealand, with her husband, the inimitable Dr. Jax, two kids and two rats. When she's not torturing alpha males and their gutsy heroines, she can be found drinking chocolate martinis, reading anything she can lay her hands on, wasting time on social media or being forced to go mountain biking with her husband. To keep up-to-date with Jackie's new releases and other news, sign up to her newsletter at jackieashenden.com.

Books by Jackie Ashenden

Harlequin Presents

The Italian's Final Redemption
The World's Most Notorious Greek
The Innocent Carrying His Legacy
The Wedding Night They Never Had
The Innocent's One-Night Proposal
The Maid the Greek Married

Pregnant Princesses

Pregnant by the Wrong Prince

Rival Billionaire Tycoons

A Diamond for My Forbidden Bride
Stolen for My Spanish Scandal

Visit the Author Profile page
at Harlequin.com for more titles.

To all those who will never pick up a
Harlequin Presents. So long, suckers!
All the more for us!

CHAPTER ONE

THE CLUB DIDN'T have a name. It didn't need one. Just as the three men lounging on the metal catwalk up above the dance floor didn't need any introductions.

Solace Ashworth knew who they were.

Kings.

They'd once been the three Wicked Princes— or so the media had dubbed them back when they'd been at Oxford university—causing mayhem wherever they went. Now they'd ascended their thrones they were wicked no longer.

Or at least one of them wasn't.

They were all tall and broad-shouldered— clearly, they fed baby kings much better than they did poor nobodies—two of them with short black hair, the third a dark, rich tawny that gleamed gold in the pulsing dance-floor lights.

The tawny-haired man was King Augustine Solari of Isavere, a mountain kingdom between

Spain and Italy, and still very, very wicked, or so the gossip columns said.

One of the black-haired men was Sheikh Khalil ibn al-Nazari of Al Da'Ira, an ancient desert kingdom on the Red Sea near Saudi Arabia. He was apparently less wicked than Augustine, though his reputation for ruthlessness was second to none.

It was the third man, though, who held Solace's attention.

He was leaning on the metal rail that bounded the catwalk, long fingers curled around it, staring down at the heaving dance floor beneath him with a single-minded focus that made Solace catch her breath.

King Galen Kouros of Kalithera, a small, picturesque country on the Adriatic coast. Where they were now.

The nameless club was in Therisos, the nation's capital, and a secret venue only open to royalty and their guests. Solace still couldn't believe they'd let her in, but the password she'd paid a lot of money for had worked, and in the silver couture dress she'd also paid a lot of money for she looked as though she belonged here.

Just as well. Because right now, desperate times called for desperate measures and the plan she was about to put in motion was surely as desperate as they came.

A plan that involved the man on the catwalk.

There were many beautiful people in the club tonight, but he was the most beautiful.

Tall and broad, with wide shoulders and lean hips, his was the classic, perfect male form, shown off to perfection by the plain black shirt and black suit trousers he wore. Simple clothes designed to highlight the beauty of the man.

His coal-black hair was worn short, revealing the perfect bone structure of his face: high cheekbones, straight nose, the most beautifully carved mouth.

Solace swallowed. She remembered—

No. She couldn't allow herself to get distracted by memories or by his beauty.

She was here for one reason and one reason only: seduce him, then blackmail him.

Her plan was mad, of course, and very wrong, but she'd been left with no choice. She'd tried contacting the Kalitheran embassy, first via email then by phone, relating her story to them and then requesting help. But they hadn't believed her. Even a personal visit to demand she see someone in authority had involved her being escorted from the premises as a nuisance. She'd briefly considered whether she could get a lawyer to help, but she didn't have the money and she'd heard enough about lawyers not to trust them anyway.

No, all she'd had was herself and this plan of hers.

Getting herself from London to Therisos had been the easy part. Even getting into this very exclusive, nameless nightclub hadn't been the hardest part.

No, the hardest part was going to be getting his attention.

The people on the dance floor were doing a very good impression of acting as if they didn't know who the three men standing above them were, though Solace noticed many sending occasional glances upwards.

Oh, yes, they knew, but the whole point of the club was discretion. Here royalty could relax and be human without fear of media reprisal, even if it was just for a night.

Up on the catwalk, King Augustine, who was standing on one side of Galen, clapped him on the shoulder and said something that made him shake his head. On the other side of Galen was Sheikh Khalil, who stood with his powerful arms folded, his attention also on the dance floor. He'd clearly said something amusing since Augustine laughed and a brief, flickering smile lit Galen's sternly beautiful face.

Solace's heart twisted. She remembered that

smile. He'd given it to her once, though she hadn't known who he was at the time. She'd been dazzled by its warmth. No one had ever smiled at her that way either before or since.

You're getting distracted again. Focus.

She gritted her teeth and ignored the ache that lurked just behind her breastbone. It didn't matter what she wanted. It didn't matter that this was going to hurt. It didn't even matter that what she was about to do was very, *very* wrong.

What mattered was getting her baby son back and for him she would do anything, anything at all.

Even blackmail a king. The king who was his father.

Gathering her courage, Solace stepped from the shadows where she'd been lurking and made her way onto the dance floor. Bodies heaved around her, lights flashing. The bass throbbed, so deep she could feel it in the soles of feet, in her chest.

She stood out. She knew she did. She'd made sure of it. The dress she wore was a confection of form-fitting silver mesh with fine silver chains for straps, and it glittered and sparkled in the light.

A dress made for getting attention.

Male heads turned as she began to dance, moving to the music in the way she'd studied through watching countless YouTube videos in her local library. Sexy and sensual, yet not too explicit. She'd prepared for this the way she prepared for everything: as if for a battle where surrender was not an option.

She didn't look up, not yet. He needed to see her first.

Familiar anxiety twisted inside her, but she ignored it with the ease of long practice. If she didn't catch his attention now, she'd think of something else. She'd done it before wearing a catering uniform and a mask; doing it wearing nothing but a silver-mesh dress was surely a piece of cake.

A couple of men were dancing near her now, which made her wary. She knew how being a woman on her own made her a target. She'd been on her own all her life and being thought of as easy prey was something she was intimately familiar with.

However, according to the thread in one of the secret Internet chatrooms she'd managed to gain access to, this club had strict rules when it came to behaviour and those rules were enforced. Sure enough the men didn't come too close, but they looked at her with interest in their eyes. Clearly the dress was doing its job.

But there was only one man whose interest she wanted.

She took a breath and finally looked up.

And froze.

He was looking straight at her.

All the air abruptly escaped her lungs in a wild rush and her skin prickled with sudden heat.

She had forgotten.

She had forgotten how the impact of his gaze was like a gut punch. How he made her feel as if she were going to go up in flames on the spot.

It had happened that night in London, too. She'd been in her uniform and incredibly nervous because it had been her first job with the catering company and a step up from waitressing and cleaning. But she'd been determined to do brilliantly, because the money had been good, and she'd had plans. She'd wanted to go back to high school and finish this time, and then, if she did well, perhaps go to university and get a law degree.

All the staff that night had been instructed to wear masks to match the guests since it had been a masquerade ball, and they'd been under strict instructions not to draw attention to themselves. She'd been moving through the crowds with a tray of full champagne flutes, pleased that so far everything seemed to be going well.

Then the tall man in the middle of a knot of people had looked up and she'd frozen the way she was freezing now. His eyes had been a dense, dark blue and she'd been caught in them like a rabbit in a trap. And an unfamiliar feeling had swept over her, a sizzling, crackling energy humming in the space between them, making her feel hot all over.

She'd been so shocked that she'd taken an instinctive step back, only to bump into someone standing behind her, which in turn had loosened her hold on the tray, sending it crashing onto the floor...

Solace's mouth was dry and despite the deafening thump of the music she could hear her heart beating loudly in her head.

Above her on the catwalk, his powerful figure had gone very still, his hands gripping the rail tightly.

Galen Kouros was famous, not only for his progressive rule and the work he'd done to improve the lives of his most severely disadvantaged subjects, but also for his spotless reputation, and in the ten years since he'd ascended the throne no hint of scandal had ever attached itself to him. He was the most straitlaced king in Europe. Even the revelation of his baby son, which had caused an initial media fuss, had been swiftly quelled by a sombre palace statement detailing the death of the King's apparent fiancée and the mother of his son, and a request for privacy at this delicate time. Which had been duly given since he was beloved by his people and the media alike.

But that statement was a lie, just as his spotless reputation was a lie.

Galen might be a touch less rigid than his father, but that wickedness he'd once been famous for as a prince was still part of him. And Solace knew because *she* was the mother of his child and there had been only wickedness when he'd taken her in that deserted office the night of that masquerade ball. A wickedness that had left her trembling with desire and desperation, and a need she'd been powerless to resist.

She'd made a mistake that night. She'd surrendered to him and the heat that had burned between them and had earned herself nothing but pain because of it. But she'd learned her lesson and she wasn't going to surrender again. *Never* again, not to anyone. No matter how beautiful or compelling or desirable they were.

Tonight, she was going to do the opposite. Tonight, she was going to be the one with the power and *he* would surrender to *her*. She would use that spotless reputation of his against him and take back the son she'd lost. The son he'd taken from her.

She was a still point in the shifting, heaving mass of dancers around her, steeling herself as she held his gaze, feeling the air between them thicken and come alive with the same burning, sizzling chemistry she'd felt that night at the gala. And that was a good thing, even though it frightened her on some deep level.

But no, she wasn't going to lose herself this time.

This time she had a purpose.

'Come and catch me, Your Majesty,' she whispered to him, even though he wouldn't be able to hear. 'Catch me if you can.'

Then she tore her gaze from his and made her way off the dance floor and deeper into the club.

'That looks like trouble,' Khalil observed coolly from his place on the catwalk beside Galen.

'Pretty trouble,' Augustine agreed.

Galen barely heard them. The woman in the silver dress had disappeared into the crowd, but he was still staring after her, conscious that he was gripping the rail very tightly, every muscle in his body tense.

He'd noticed her immediately. It had been impossible not to. Everyone else in the club was wearing dark shades or black, but not her. She'd stood out in the crowd like the only star in a night sky, glittering and bright in a dress that seemed to be made out of liquid mercury. Her long, straight pale hair had swirled like a veil around her as she'd danced, graceful and sensual. She looked as if she'd been dipped in silver, moonlight in the shape of a woman.

His wasn't the only attention she'd drawn, others had obviously been as taken with her as he was, moving to dance closer to her, and he'd been filled with a wave of possessiveness that had nearly made him stride from the catwalk and down the stairs to join her on the dance floor. Make it clear to every man in the club that she was his.

A ridiculous notion. He'd never been a possessive man and he wasn't about to start being one over a pretty stranger in a club. He wasn't here to find a woman anyway. He was here to meet his friends and that was all.

Except he didn't stop scanning the crowds below him, searching for a flash of silver.

'I take it you're going to go after her?' Augustine murmured.

'No,' Galen said.

'Are you sure? Because if you're not going to then I might—'

'No,' Galen repeated and found he'd pushed himself away from the rail and was now standing on the catwalk eye to eye with one of his closest friends. 'You will not.'

But the expression on Augustine's fallen-angel face was only amused. 'Does that sound like a claim to you, Khal?' he said, not looking away from Galen.

'It does,' Khalil agreed. He didn't sound amused. He sounded cool and unruffled, the way he always did.

Laughter glittered in Augustine's blue-green eyes and probably at Galen's expense, but Galen ignored it. He was long used to his friend's tendency to poke at people to get a reaction. It was useful, or so Augustine claimed. You could tell a lot about a person by how long they held onto their temper.

Galen never lost his, never even let it slip. A loose temper was a sign of a weak mind, his father had often said, which Galen had always thought the worst kind of hypocrisy. Because while Alexandros Kouros had never screamed or shouted, his cold fury had consumed not only his court, but also Galen's childhood into the bargain.

Galen himself tried to be a different sort of king, a less rigid king, but there was only so much he could do given the bitter truth that lay at the heart of his throne. A secret only he knew, that no one else could ever find out.

It was guarding that secret that made him act in ways that made him rather too much like Alexandros for comfort.

Not that he had a choice.

'Not now, August,' Galen said flatly. 'I'm not in the mood.'

Augustine gave him an assessing look. 'Forgive me, my friend, but when are you in the mood?'

'That's none of your—'

'You're in danger of becoming as boring as your reputation, Galen, I told you this.' A light thread of amusement coloured his voice, but there was a hint of steel beneath it too. Augustine was very fond of the iron fist in the velvet glove approach.

Galen was conscious of a flick of irritation. It was his friends' last night in Therisos—they'd both come for a brief, unofficial visit to catch up, which the three of them did every three months or when their schedules allowed—and Augustine had wanted to mark the occasion by visiting the club. It was a chain he'd set up himself, mainly for his own amusement, or so he'd said, but also because he was sick of being photographed everywhere he went and preferred a more…discreet environment.

There were no reporters here and everyone who entered signed an NDA. The perfect place to let your hair down, or so Augustine had said. 'Remember your youth,' he'd also said. 'You could afford to be a little more wicked, Galen.'

But his youth was something Galen had no

wish to revisit and being a little more wicked was the one thing he could *not* afford, especially not after the mistake he'd made the previous year. The mistake that had ended with a son Galen had never known he'd had until after he was born.

Galen would fight to the death for Leo, but that mistake? He would not make it again. He *could* not make it again.

'I do not care what you think of my reputation.' He tried to sound as cool as Khal, but it came out sounding more of a growl than anything else. 'I'm not chasing after some stranger just because you think I need to be less boring.'

He's right though. You know what happens when you deny yourself.

Yes, he did. But that only meant he had to try harder.

Augustine shrugged. 'A woman like that isn't going home alone tonight, but I suppose it's your choice. If you don't want her, someone else will.'

Galen knew what his friend was doing, the manipulative bastard. 'I don't care,' he said.

'Do you not?' Augustine raised a brow and glanced over Galen's shoulder at Khalil. 'What about you, Khal? Maybe for yourself?'

The Sheikh, whose mere word in Al Da'Ira was law, looked thoughtful. 'She is…exquisite. Maybe I could—'

'No,' Galen said for the third time. 'Not you as well.'

Khalil only gazed blandly back, his expression inscrutable.

His friends meant well, Galen knew that, but there were reasons he had to behave with the utmost discretion wherever he went. Kostas, his uncle, watched him, waiting for one slip, and while Galen had successfully managed him the past ten years since he'd been crowned, Leo's birth had complicated things, making Kostas even more suspicious than he already was.

Kostas would love to see him have to abdicate and take the throne for himself.

Except Galen would never allow that to happen. It was why he couldn't let go his control over his baser appetites, not even for a moment. He couldn't give Kostas any reason to question him.

The safety of his country depended on it.

But there are no reporters here. No one will tell. And you have not been with a woman in so long. Not since—

Ah, but he wasn't going to think of that night when his son was conceived. Where he'd put at risk everything, including his throne, for passion with a nameless woman at a masquerade ball of all things.

He couldn't allow it to happen again, no matter how hungry his body was.

The woman in silver was exquisite, as Khalil had said, but he wasn't going to go chasing after her. He had a million things to do, a king always did, but one of the things on his list was finding himself a wife. The kings of Kalithera always chose someone from the aristocracy, of a good family since family was important, and he already had a list of candidates. He hoped he'd have chemistry with at least one of them, which would mean he could sate his hunger with her, not some nameless stranger in a nightclub.

'Fine,' Augustine said in a long-suffering tone. 'If you want to deny yourself then on your head be it. But I'm certainly not going to.'

No, but then Augustine wouldn't. He never denied himself anything.

Galen stepped away from the rail. 'Amuse yourself however you like, gentlemen. I have some more work to do tonight.'

Augustine only shook his head, while Khalil gave him a long, expressionless look that Galen knew full well was Khal trying to understand what he was up to.

Well, the answer to that was nothing. He'd had enough of this club, and he was leaving, the woman in silver be damned.

Striding along the catwalk, he came to the

stairs and descended into the crowds. His security detail shifted from the various discreet places where they'd been waiting, ready to come with him. Augustine and Khalil hadn't brought theirs tonight, but Galen always had his attend. Kostas would have noticed if he'd left them behind and started asking questions as to why, and Galen didn't want him asking those questions. Since Leo had arrived on the scene, he'd had to be extra cautious. His security were all intensely loyal to him and no man amongst them would have let slip anything, but he couldn't be too careful. If nothing else, last year's catastrophe had proved that.

The spotlights pulsed as he headed towards the exit and a flash of silver caught his eye. He stopped, searching instinctively for the location of that flash.

There she was, standing against a wall in the darkest part of the club, the strobing lights catching the glitter of her dress. It moulded to her figure like molten silver, outlining the most delicious curves he'd ever seen. Full breasts, a neat waist, generous hips...

His fingers itched. He wanted to touch her, run his hands over her, slip the delicate chains holding up that dress off her shoulders and watch as the fabric fell down to reveal all those luscious curves.

But no. Those were old habits. He'd already decided he wasn't going to indulge himself tonight, no matter what Augustine thought. And while she was certainly lovely, this woman wasn't going to make him change his mind no matter how delicious she was.

Yet he didn't move, slowly becoming aware that the woman wasn't alone. A man was with her, leaning over her, and from out of nowhere came a short, sharp burst of territorial anger.

She is your prey tonight.

Prey? Ridiculous. His days of prowling through the clubs purely for the thrill of the chase and the adrenaline rush of a one-night stand were over, as were the forbidden parties that sometimes turned into orgies and the stupid, drunken stunts he, Khal and Augustine used to pull, causing the kind of mayhem that only three young men with too much money and far too much arrogance could. At least until his father had had a stroke, and he'd been called back to Kalithera, and he'd had to put all of that behind him.

He still remembered going into his father's bedroom the night he'd returned to Therisos. Alexandros had barely been able to speak, but Galen had understood him well enough: the media storm that had erupted after Galen had been at a party with under-age girls had been the last straw. That had proved he was unfit to take the crown of Kalithera and so he was being disowned in favour of Kostas, his uncle.

Galen had always known his father had hated him, the old man had made it quite clear throughout the entirety of his childhood, and even though he'd tried to tell Alexandros that he'd had nothing to do with those girls, Alexandros hadn't listened.

And then Galen had promptly forgotten all about the girls, because then Alexandros had dealt his second, more devasting blow: Galen's mother, who'd died not long after having him, had had an affair with a palace servant nine months before Galen was born. Galen might not be Alexandros's son after all.

The shock had rendered him mute. His entire childhood had been a constant battle to please a man who'd never been satisfied with anything Galen had done, who'd punished him for the smallest infractions and for no reason. Who'd constantly seemed furious with him… It all now made sense.

Not that knowing the truth made any difference. Not when in the end Galen had given up. Given up trying to be good, given up trying to obey Alexandros's seemingly pointless rules. Given up wanting to follow in the footsteps of a man who'd loathed the very sight of him. He'd even given up wanting to be Alexandros's heir...

All that trying had been for nothing. He might be another man's son.

Galen would have found it a relief in its way, if his father hadn't named his brother, Galen's uncle, as the new heir. Kostas had always been a moral vacuum, constantly pandering to his big-business cronies, and had spent years trying to get Alexandros to make Kalithera a tax haven. He'd already influenced Alexandros to pass policies that favoured the rich, ignoring the very real poverty of some of the Kalitheran people.

Alexandros had made no secret of the fact that he thought his so-called son would make an unfit king, and since Galen had found his father's training for the role...difficult, he'd sometimes wondered if there wasn't some truth to that.

Yet even so, he couldn't let Kostas take the crown. It was wrong to take a throne that might not be his, but there was no other heir, and no one else to protect Kalithera.

There was only him.

An imperfect king he might be, but Galen hadn't seen another choice. So when his father had died before he could change the succession, Galen had claimed the throne. Of course, one DNA test would have proven conclusively who he was once and for all, but he couldn't take the risk. If it turned out he wasn't Alexandros's son, he would have to abdicate in favour of Kostas, who would then run Kalithera into the ground.

His uncle hadn't known all of Alexandros's plans to name him the heir, but he'd always been a suspicious man and had known Alexandros hadn't thought much of Galen, and every so often there had been mutterings about Galen's past and how he was unfit to rule. And while Galen had cemented his role as King over the past ten years, he couldn't allow Kostas's mutterings to take hold and foster doubt.

He had to be careful. To behave in such a way as to not draw attention, not put a foot out of line, not to remind his uncle of past behaviour that he'd left behind. Not remind anyone—especially not the media—of the Wicked Prince he'd once been.

And he'd been very successful so far. He'd managed to keep himself and Kalithera out of the headlines for the past ten years. Until that mistake he'd made last year with that woman, that exceptional, lovely woman with clear, piercing grey eyes and the gut punch of a chemistry that he hadn't been able to resist.

It was a flaw of his, one of his greatest, that he found controlling his baser urges so difficult.

Which was why he had to try even harder not
to fall prey to them.

Yet a similar chemistry was hitting him now,
crackling over his skin as he watched her, along
with a growing need to stride over to where she
stood and take that interloper by the scruff of
his neck and jerk him away from her.

As the man leaned further in towards her, she
glanced away, turning her head in Galen's direction. Their eyes met and, as he had up on that
catwalk, he felt the shock of desire right down
low inside him, raw and primal, and he was
moving in her direction before he even knew
what he was doing.

She saw him before the man standing in front
of her did, her eyes going wide. Her partner,
obviously picking up on her shift in attention,
looked in Galen's direction too, but after seeing who it was coming towards them he went
pale and took a step away from her before dis-
appearing into the crowd.

Galen should have stopped then. He should
have turned around and left himself.

But he didn't.

The woman didn't move. She drew him in
like a magnet, watching him come closer, her
eyes dark and wide. He could see the pulse at
the base of her throat beating hard and fast, the
light shimmering over the fabric of her dress

betraying her quickened breathing. She wasn't exactly beautiful—her nose was too long, and her mouth was too wide—yet there was something mesmerising about her face, something that caught his attention and held it. She seemed familiar in some way, though he couldn't put his finger on why. He'd never met her before, he was sure.

She didn't say anything as he came to a stop in front of her, only looked up at him. Her mouth was full and lovely, her lashes thick and blonde, a startling contrast to her dark eyes. And in those dark eyes a fire burned.

A fire that found an answering spark inside him.

He didn't know what had made him come over to her and he didn't know why he was standing in front of her now, when what he'd fully intended was to leave. This was a mistake, and he knew it, yet he stayed where he was, feeling the flames inside him start to leap.

'Did you want something?' she asked in English. Her voice had a pleasing husk to it that shivered over his skin like a caress. 'I mean, you frightened off that guy for a reason, I presume?' She didn't sound as if she minded her prospective partner being frightened off in the least.

Anger coiled inside him, at himself and what he was doing, and his apparent inability to walk away, and at that tantalising hint of familiarity that he couldn't quite pinpoint. But anger was an emotion he didn't allow himself, so he crushed it. Hard.

'Who are you?' he asked.

Her gaze flickered yet she didn't move. She was leaning back against the wall, almost as if she was trying to put distance between them, yet he wasn't standing that close. She could have moved away if she'd chosen.

'That depends.' The pulse at the base of her throat was beating faster now. He wanted to put his mouth there and taste it. 'Who wants to know?'

Galen ignored the question, taking a step closer as he searched her lovely face, caught in the grip of a compulsion he could hardly explain even to himself. 'You are familiar,' he murmured. 'Have we met?'

'Oh, I don't think so.' Her gaze met his from underneath her lashes. 'I think I would have remembered you.'

And he would have remembered her…oh, yes, he would.

He took another step. 'What is your name?'

'Why should I tell you?' The light shimmered across the silver fabric of her dress, and she raised one blonde brow. 'Your Majesty.'

A challenging woman. Oh, he liked that. He

liked that very much. She knew who he was and yet from the heated glitter in her eyes, she was not intimidated by him. Not at all.

It's been a long time. Too long.

Over a whole year and still he thought about that night at the ball with the beautiful grey-eyed woman. She'd had no idea who he was. With her he'd been just a man and she'd wanted that man so passionately.

As if it didn't matter what a liar you are...

Galen ignored the thought. That night was over and the woman—Solace had been her name, he'd discovered later—long gone. But tonight...well, this woman was right in front of him, and the night was still young, and maybe Augustine had been right. Maybe he did need to let the leash off. He'd make sure Kostas wouldn't know and, besides, he knew from experience that abstinence only made things harder. Every so often it was necessary to let off steam in order to prevent any more mistakes, and if this woman was here and she wanted him...

Galen took another step to test her. There were only inches between them now, and he could smell her subtle scent, warm female flesh and the sweetness of lilies.

She didn't move, only watched him, so slowly he put one hand on the wall beside her head and then, after a moment, did the same with the other, caging her.

There was no alarm in her dark eyes, only that burning flame, that heat. Reminding him that he wasn't just a king, but a man as well, and that man was hungry. No, that man was starving.

Her gaze dropped to his mouth and his body hardened instantly, the warmth of her intoxicating.

Yes. It seemed she *was* interested after all.

Theos, he hadn't felt this intensely about a woman in years. If he ever had.

You did, remember?

No, he was not going to think of her. He would obliterate the memory of her piercing grey eyes and the silver flames that had burned in them with this woman. Now. Tonight.

'Feel free to leave.' He leaned in, inhaling her, his lips almost but not quite brushing hers. 'At any time.'

It was then that he realised she was trembling. Yet it wasn't with fright.

Because her gaze lifted from his mouth, and he felt the moment she locked eyes with him. The impact was almost physical.

Then abruptly she leaned forward and kissed him.

CHAPTER TWO

SOLACE KNEW SHE had to be the one to make the first move. It was vital in keeping him off balance so he wouldn't recognise her, not to mention making sure the power stayed with her. Because she wasn't going to let him take control, not again. Not the way he had that night at the ball, when he'd overwhelmed her first with unexpected kindness, and then with passion. Her life had been turned on its head in that moment, leaving all her careful plans for a future in ruins.

Before him, she'd been a woman who'd finally got her crappy life in order and was starting to think that maybe, just maybe she *could* have all the things she'd wanted back when she'd been a lonely girl in the foster system.

Then he'd come along and shown her the one thing her life had been missing—his touch. And her glittering future had gone up in smoke.

But it was going to be different this time, because this time *she* was in control. This time *she* was going to upend his life the way he'd up-ended hers, and she was going to take back the one good thing he'd given her: her son.

Galen had come after her as she'd hoped he would, but now she had to steel herself and keep her head, not let the powerful current of their physical chemistry wash her away.

Yet the moment her lips touched his, she could feel that steel begin to fracture.

The way he stood in front of her, looming over her, his arms on either side, caging her in. Surrounding her with his heat and his scent. Blocking out the rest of the nightclub, blocking out the entire world…

It had been like that that night, when he'd held her against the wall in the deserted office, his powerful body between her and the world, making her feel protected and safe. It had been an intoxicating experience for a woman who'd never felt either of those things before, not in her entire life.

He made her feel that way now and she hated it. Because it was a lie. He hadn't protected her, and he hadn't saved her. He'd taken her to heaven and back, then delivered her straight to hell.

It wasn't all his fault. You ran away. Then you signed those papers, remember?

But she didn't want to remember. Not about how she'd run after their encounter or about the papers his representatives from Kalithera had thrust at her that first night out of hospital. Papers that she'd signed, giving up her maternal rights to her own child.

She *never* wanted to remember that, or the black hole of postnatal depression she'd fallen into after they'd taken her baby away, a bleakness that had taken hold of her soul. She'd had no one to talk to, no one to tell her she'd done the right thing giving her baby away. No one to reassure her that eventually the horrifying guilt over what she'd done would one day go away.

No, she was stronger now, she was in charge now, and she wouldn't let herself get overwhelmed by anything or anyone ever again.

Except then he closed what little distance remained between them, crushing her against the wall, and the steel inside her fractured a little more.

Oh, she remembered this. How he was so hot, like iron, and how glorious he'd felt. He was so much bigger than she was, so much more powerful. He could protect her from harm. And he was so hungry.

All for her.

She'd grown up in a dozen foster homes and apart from Katherine, the one foster mum who'd

ever taken an interest, no one had looked out
for her, no one had even noticed her. No one
had cared.

Now you have a king desperate to have you.

Her senses reeled. His mouth was hot, exploring her with a rough mastery that left her trembling even harder than she had been already.

She'd thought she'd be ecstatic that he'd come
after her, and she was. But she was also afraid.
Afraid of what she felt and how easily he could
overturn her conviction if she let him.

So? Don't let him.

Solace put a hand on his chest and pushed at
him, her breath coming in short, hard gasps.

He lifted his head instantly, the expression on his perfect face taut and hungry, but
he didn't move away. The look in his hot blue
eyes burned.

She'd done her research. She'd watched as
many videos of him as she could, at official
events and with his subjects, or the occasional,
rare interview, and he was always cool and polite and courteous. There had been a distance
to him, as if he was keeping himself apart, but
there was no distance at all to him now.

Just as there hadn't been any distance fifteen
months earlier.

He was not the King now, he was a man, and
he burned for her.

She felt dizzy. His warm, woody scent was all around her, and the feel of his hard chest pressed against her sensitive breasts made the low pulse of desire pulse even harder.

'Do you want me to stop?' His gaze was fierce, demanding. 'Because if so, you need to tell me immediately.'

'No,' she forced out, trying to get some air into her lungs. 'I just needed a…a moment.'

He stared at her so intently she felt as if he were seeing inside her head. 'But you don't need one now, do you?'

She did need one now. She needed more than one. She needed to get out of here, get away from him before she lost herself again, yet running wouldn't get her what she wanted.

Besides, you want a taste of him again, don't deny it. A taste of how good he can make you feel.

'No,' she made herself say, both to him and to the voice in her head. 'No, I don't.'

Without a word, he bent, his breath warm on her skin as he brushed his mouth along the line of her jaw. Then he kissed her again, hot and raw and deep, making her go up in flames once more.

Making her remember that night again, and how, when he'd kissed her, she'd lost her mind. She'd never been kissed before, never been touched, or at least not by a man and certainly not for pleasure, and she'd had no idea how good it would feel. That precious half-hour she'd had with him had been…incandescent.

It was incandescent now.

She moaned, the taste of him dark chocolate and sin, the good Scotch she used to steal from that one foster father's drinks cabinet, the flavour of the forbidden, all the delicious things she could never afford to have for herself. It was wrong to want this, especially given who he was and the trap she'd fallen into the last time, but she was finding it difficult to remember why resisting him was so important in the first place.

Because it nearly destroyed you the last time and you can't go through that again.

Everything in her tensed in response. It was true, she couldn't. She had to resist him, she *had* to.

Then his long fingers wrapped around her throat in a firm, dominant hold, and all that tension began to bleed away, as if something inside her had finally stopped struggling and given in to the inevitable.

All her life she'd been on her own. She'd never belonged to anyone. But right here, right now, with his hand on her throat, she felt as if she belonged to him.

The man who took your baby from you.

She barely heard the thought this time as he gentled the kiss, nipping at her bottom lip and tracing the shape of it with his tongue, his thumb stroking the side of her neck.

'I won't hurt you,' he breathed in her ear. 'You're safe with me.' He shifted his hips in a subtle movement, the hard ridge behind his fly pressing against the heat between her thighs, nudging the most exquisitely sensitive part of her and making her tremble. 'But I want you. I want you to come home with me.'

It was what she'd hoped for. She'd spent the blood money the Kalitherans had given her in return for her son on her dress and flights to Kalithera, and not a little of it had also gone to various people she'd contacted who had inside knowledge on Galen's schedule.

She'd planned for this meticulously and it was all coming together. She'd even hoped that their chemistry would be just as strong, because to tempt a man like him, she'd need it to be. And she'd assumed that resisting him herself would be easy, that the lure of her son would be enough inducement not to surrender.

But it wasn't easy. It wasn't.

There was a warm, pulsing ache between her thighs and a different sort of ache behind her breastbone, a longing she couldn't get rid of no matter how hard she tried. He'd seduced her completely once and if she wasn't careful, he might again, and that wasn't how it was supposed to happen.

Does it matter? Why not surrender to him? It's only physical and you would enjoy it.

She would. She could go home with him, be his lover for the night, then take some incriminating pictures and blackmail him with them. Tell him that if he didn't give her son back, she'd release them to the press. And she couldn't take those pictures if she wasn't in his bed. Yet none of that meant she couldn't have a little something for herself. Some pleasure before all the unpleasantness. She was allowed, surely? After all the months of crushing guilt and aching loneliness? All the months of agony?

'Well?' He was exploring the line of her lower lip, brushing soft kisses along it as he shifted his other hand from beside her head, his fingers dropping to slide beneath one of the chains holding her dress up, pulling at it gently so the material tightened over her achingly sensitive nipples. 'Yes or no?' He stroked down over the chain, over the silver mesh of her dress and down, tracing the curve of her breast.

She felt almost drunk, as if she'd swallowed four cocktails in quick succession. Then those wicked fingers brushed across one nipple, sending sparks cascading through her, making her gasp yet again. Only to have his mouth cover hers and swallow the sound, the sensual brush of his tongue against hers making a low moan of need vibrate in her throat.

'Is that a yes?' he murmured, his finger-tips now exploring her collarbones with aching lightness.

She could barely speak, having to force out the word. 'Y-Yes.'

He pulled back a fraction and stared down at her. 'You can trust me.'

You can't ever trust him. Not after what happened.

No, she already knew that. But all she was going to trust him with tonight was her body. The rest of her she would keep safely locked away. She just had to remember who this was all for: her son.

Very deliberately, Solace placed her hands on the warm cotton that covered his chest. 'Then take me home, Your Majesty.'

An intense blue flame leapt in his eyes that stole her breath. 'Galen. You may call me Galen.' Then he pushed himself away from her and grabbed her hand, threading his fingers through hers. And without a word, he turned and led her out of the club.

Her legs were shaky, and she almost stumbled a couple of times, catching herself at the last minute. He didn't stop and he didn't turn, obviously desperate to get her away.

And you're desperate to follow. The way you were last time.

But Solace ignored the voice. It wouldn't be like last time. She hadn't known what she was doing back then, but she did now. And this time she had a purpose. This time she'd take the physical pleasure without letting herself become lost in it.

The club's exit was in a different place from its entrance for the added privacy of its patrons, so when she and Galen stepped outside it was into a narrow cobbled street, surrounded by the jumble of whitewashed buildings so typical of Therisan architecture. The street was quiet and empty, bathed in the sulphurous glow of the streetlights, the low hum of the old city—traffic and people and, beyond that, the sound of the sea—murmuring in the background.

A sleek black limo waited at the kerb. Galen's security team came out of the club behind them and moved into formation, walking beside her and Galen as he strode to the car, pulling her along with him. One of the men darted ahead and opened the limo door, and then she was bundled inside, Galen following behind her.

The door slammed shut, cutting off the noise of the city completely.

'Don't worry,' Galen murmured. 'The windows are tinted. No one can see in.' He leaned forward and pressed a button, so the divider rose between them and the driver. 'Now,' he went on as they were finally enclosed in the back seat and completely private. 'Where were we?'

Then he reached for her and pulled her into his lap, positioning her so she was sitting astride him, facing him, her legs spread on either side of his lean hips, her knees pressed into the soft black leather of the seat.

The limo had begun to move, she could feel it, light from outside shining through the windows and flickering over his perfect face. His body was hot and very hard, his expression fierce. The blue of his eyes had darkened into midnight, and they glittered as he swept a glance down over the shimmering silver mesh of her dress.

He dropped his hands to the chains holding it up and her breath caught as his fingers slid beneath them, stroking her skin and making her shiver. 'You're wearing too many clothes.'

Her heartbeat was too loud, the touch of his fingers sending shudders through her. This was happening so fast, and she didn't know how to slow it down. Then again, maybe that was a good thing. Fast didn't give her time to think or to second-guess, or for him to latch onto that familiarity again.

'Then maybe you should do something about it,' she said breathlessly.

That hot blue gaze roamed over her face. 'You like giving orders, hmm?'

'You're talking too much.' She barely knew what she was saying, shifting on his rock-hard thighs, unable to keep still.

'Is that so?' A fleeting amusement glittered in his eyes, only to be replaced by something much more intense. 'I am a king, silver girl. And kings do not obey orders. They give them.'

Then, without waiting for her to speak, he eased the chains off her shoulders.

She made no move to stop him, shivering as the fabric slipped down to her waist, baring her, and then shivering even harder as his gaze swept over her, flaring with hunger.

It sharpened her own, made it bloom inside her like a flower. She'd never thought she'd want a man's attention, but he'd proved her wrong the last time and he proved her wrong now.

She did want a man's attention, *his* attention, so she made no effort to cover herself, even though she'd never been naked in front of any-one before. And when he took her wrists in a firm but gentle grip, guiding them to the small of her back and holding them there with one hand, she didn't protest.

His gaze swept down her body once more and he made no effort to hide his appreciation. 'You're beautiful.'

Unexpectedly, her throat closed. This was different. When he'd had her against the wall in that deserted office, both of them had been too desperate to bother with words. She hadn't known who he was. All she'd known was that his blue eyes seemed to see her soul and his touch had set her on fire.

But now she was half naked and there was time to speak, and she realised a part of her had been waiting for him to either recognise her or discover he'd made a mistake, that he didn't want her after all. Yet apparently neither of those things were true.

No one had ever called her beautiful before.

She'd told herself many times over the years since Katherine had changed her mind about adopting her that she didn't need or want anyone to care. She didn't need their attention or their notice.

Except a part of her did, and that part was unfurling under his gaze like a snowdrop at the first hint of the sun.

As if he could read her mind, his gaze narrowed. 'What is it?'

She turned her head away in an instinctive effort to hide the traitorous feeling, only for strong fingers to grip her chin and turn her back to face him.

'You don't like being called beautiful?' That blue gaze of his sharp as a spear.

Great. The last thing she needed was an interrogation. This was supposed to be fast and frantic, sex with a nameless stranger he took home for a one-night stand. He was not supposed to be interested in her feelings.

But he was the last time.

Solace swallowed, remembering the horror as she'd stared at the broken glass and champagne covering the floor of the ballroom, knowing she'd be fired. And how she'd gone to her knees, trying to clean up the mess herself, only to hear a deep, calm voice giving orders. And when she'd looked up, those deep, mesmerising blue eyes had been on hers. 'Come with me,' he'd said quietly, holding out a hand. 'This will all be cleaned up. I will see to it personally.' Of all the people staring at her and the mess she'd created, he was the only one who'd helped her. Who'd taken her hand and led her off to the side of the ballroom so she could compose herself.

His gaze had been just as piercing then as it was now. Seeing into her. Seeing *her*.

He'll recognise you if you're not careful and then you'll never see your baby again.

No. *No.* That wasn't going to happen.

'What did I say about talking too much?' She shifted again, trying to distract him. 'You're ruining the mood.'

His eyes widened a fraction, but his grip on her chin firmed. 'Oh? Am I indeed?'

Her breath caught. She didn't know why that had snagged his interest or why he cared. What did her reaction matter? She needed to get him back on track.

She let her gaze drift to his mouth and back up again. 'Sorry, I didn't mean it. I'm just... impatient.'

Whether he believed her or not, she didn't know, the look on his face impossible to read. But his grip tightened, and he leaned in, his mouth brushing across hers in a feather-light kiss. 'I think you did mean it. And I think you don't like me calling you beautiful.' He let go of her jaw and turned his hand over, running the backs of his fingers lightly over the curve of one bare breast. 'I want to know why.'

Solace shuddered at the touch, her skin tightening, heat washing through her. He watched her fiercely, a man used to being given answers when he demanded them. A king used to being obeyed.

'Does it matter? I don't think you wanted to take me home just to talk.'

'That's true, I didn't.' He gently traced the curve of her breast, making her shift and tremble. 'But you intrigue me.'

Her mouth was dry, goosebumps rising wherever he touched, and it was becoming almost impossible to think straight. But he could not find her intriguing. That would lead to him looking at her even more intently and perhaps thinking more about why she was familiar.

She couldn't risk him remembering her, not yet. Not before she was ready.

'I'm not that interesting.' She arched into his hand, encouraging him to keep touching her. 'Please...'

'Hmm. I would disagree.' His fingers opened, cupping her breast with such delicacy she gasped. 'Tell me. How long has it been for you?'

She was shaking now. His palm burned her tender skin and when his thumb brushed over her nipple, she had to bite her lip to stop the cry that threatened to escape. Every thought she had was concentrated on his hand, on his fingers, stroking and squeezing gently, sending sharp, bright electric shocks of pleasure through her.

How long? Why was he asking her that?

'How long since what?' Her voice was uneven and breathy.

'Since anyone took their time with you. Since anyone seduced you.'

'I don't need... I don't n-need seducing.'

He leaned forward again, his mouth brushing over the side of her neck. 'Liar.' His lips were soft and warm on her skin. 'I think you want someone to take their time with you. I think you crave it. I think you're desperate to be seduced, slowly and carefully and with great attention to detail.'

He kissed his way to her throat while his thumb brushed back and forth over her nipple, making her twist and arch in his lap.

'I don't.' She was barely aware of speaking, the words coming out broken and breathless. 'I don't... I don't want that.'

His grip on her wrists loosened, his palm pressing against her back at the same time as his other hand cupped her breast. Then the heat of his mouth closed around her nipple, applying pressure.

Solace gasped as the most exquisite pleasure rushed through her, every thought in her head steadily being eroded by the pull of his mouth and the press of his hand. By the hard ridge she could feel beneath her and the strength of his grip.

There was a reason she was here with him. A very good reason. And there was something she'd planned to do later, something that was bad, but that she didn't have a choice about.

Yet she couldn't remember what that was, and she didn't want to remember. Everything was always a battle, but the past year had been so awful. There had been no escape from the guilt and the regret, and this…him…everything he did was urging her to surrender, to give in to the pleasure.

You weren't supposed to surrender, remember?

No, but she could surrender to this. It was too strong, and she just couldn't fight it any more.

So, she didn't, arching into his mouth, her trembling fingers pushing into his thick, silky black hair.

He must have sensed her give in, because he made a low growling sound as she touched him, and then she was on her back, laid lengthways across the seat, and he was over her, tugging her dress the rest of the way off, leaving her naked but for the tiny, lacy thong and her stiletto sandals.

His gaze was electric, staring down into hers, his long, powerful body settling between her thighs. 'I want you,' he said roughly. 'Now. Here. I can't wait.'

She was panting, the sound loud and gasping

in the enclosed space of the car. 'I thought you were going to seduce me.'

'I was.' He bent and nuzzled against her throat, sucking gently, making her shake. 'But you're driving me mad and right now I need to be inside you.'

He wasn't the only one being driven mad. His mouth on her skin and the shift of his hips between her thighs was making her insane. 'Yes,' she said thickly. 'Oh, God, yes, *please.*'

It happened quickly.

He clawed his trousers open and dealt with the protection. Then he shoved aside her underwear and was pushing inside her, sinking deep, making both of them groan.

Her heartbeat had gone wild, her breath coming in short, ragged gasps. The feel of him inside her almost too much. He was big, stretching her in the most exquisite way. She could barely stand it.

'Ah, God, you feel good,' he growled against her throat. 'Hot, tight, wet...everything I wanted.' He drew his hips back, nearly sliding all the way out of her before pushing back in, hard and deep. 'And tonight, you're *mine.*'

That last word echoed in her head, and she clutched at it instinctively like a talisman. Yes, she wanted to be his. She wanted to belong to him. He was everywhere, crushing her into the seat of the car, buried deep inside her, his hands beside her head. And she was back in that deserted office, held against the wall, fireworks exploding behind her eyes, for the first time in her life feeling as if she mattered, at least enough to be given this incredible ecstasy.

It had been good back then, but now, held beneath him, his darkened blue gaze holding her fast, it was...transcendent.

Beneath him, no one could touch her. No one could get to her.

She was safe from the world, and she wanted to stay here for ever.

Then he moved again, and Solace was lost.

She clutched at his back, her nails digging into the black cotton of his shirt, every thought in her head crushed by the weight of the pleasure. She lifted her hips, needing more, and he responded, catching her behind the knee and drawing one leg up and around his waist so he could slide deeper.

She groaned, pleasure crackling through her, lighting her up from inside. 'Oh, Galen...that's so good.' The words spilled out of her in a rush. 'Please, more... Please...'

But he knew, moving faster, driving her into the leather seat as he thrust harder, deeper, devouring her mouth like a starving man. She wasn't alone in her desperation. She could feel the need in him, in his accelerated breathing and the tension in his muscles, in the low, hungry sounds he made as he moved.

And it came to her dimly that there was power in surrendering to him and to this heat they generated between them.

You could destroy him.

The thought was fleeting, ripped away as the storm built inside her, the weight of the pleasure increasing, pulling taut as a bowstring between them. Then he grabbed her hand and pushed it down between them, pressing her fingers against her own slick flesh as he drove himself inside her, and the orgasm burst over her like a monsoon rain. She only had time to hear his low roar of release before she too was lost in the flood.

At first Galen was conscious of nothing but the most intense feeling of satisfaction spreading through him. But slowly, as reality began to assert itself once more, he became aware of something else, something colder and sharper.

He'd lost control.

When she'd kissed him back in the club, everything had gone out of his head. All he'd been able to think about was how quickly he could get her back to the extremely private residence he sometimes used when he needed a break from the fishbowl that was the palace. Once there, he'd been going to draw things out deliciously with a glass of wine and flirt with her a little, because he'd once loved a flirtation and, since he'd decided he was going to allow himself this one night, he was going to allow himself everything. Only then, would he seduce her.

Yet he'd done none of those things. The moment her fingers had pushed into his hair, and he'd sensed her surrender to him, he'd had her on her back and had been inside her in seconds flat.

The anger he'd felt at himself and his own weakness earlier twisted inside him once again, disturbing the heavy post-orgasmic warmth.

Theos, what was wrong with him?

You know what's wrong with you. What's always been wrong with you.

Galen shoved that thought to the darkest corner of his mind. He couldn't afford self-doubt. For the past ten years he'd ruled well enough, and, apart from that one instance last year, he'd managed to keep his own weaknesses firmly under control, conducting himself with restraint whatever the occasion.

The issue was this woman. This woman and the chemistry that burned hot and strong between them. He hadn't experienced anything like it, not since…

She stirred beneath him, giving a little wriggle before pushing at his chest. He shifted to give her some room, propping himself up on one elbow so he could look down at her.

Since that night a year ago.

It was true. Though she was different from the woman who'd caught his interest so completely that night. That woman's hair had been tightly pulled back from her forehead and pinned into a bun, not that he'd taken that much notice of her hair when it had been her grey eyes that had struck him like lightning, setting him ablaze.

The woman who lay beneath him now had pale hair and it was spread over the black leather of the car seat like white silk, and the eyes that looked up into his were dark as midnight. An unusual combination with her pale skin, currently flushed a deep and pretty rose from the pleasure he'd given her.

She'd had pale skin too, remember? And she looked at you just the way this woman is looking at you now.

Yes, but many women had pale skin, and that look of wide-eyed wonder was something he was familiar with. He was a king, after all, and that intimidated people.

Yet he couldn't shake that strange sense of familiarity.

'What?' she asked, the colour deepening in her cheeks.

He didn't reply immediately, still studying her. Where had he seen her? Surely if he'd met her before, he'd have remembered.

He brushed a strand of pale hair off her forehead. 'You don't like me looking at you, do you?'

'I'm fine with it.' Yet her gaze flickered, her lashes sweeping down as if trying to hide her expression.

Interesting. Clearly, she was not fine with it. Which was strange, given the dress she wore was designed to attract attention. And just before, in his lap, she'd been so hungry for him, and impatient, yet when he'd called her beautiful, she'd seemed uncomfortable.

Her kiss was unpractised, too.

The sharp, cold feeling wound deeper. Back in the club, she'd pulled him in for that kiss and every thought had vanished from his head. Her mouth had been almost unbearably sweet, before turning hungry and desperate after he'd taken control.

He hadn't noticed how hesitant she'd seemed. He hadn't noticed anything except her scent and the warmth of her skin, and how badly he'd wanted to touch her, bury himself inside her.

If she was indeed unpractised, you shouldn't

*have dragged her into the limo and had sex
with her.*

Galen shifted uncomfortably. Even before, as
a stupid young man determined to push as many
boundaries as he could, throw his father's suffocating upbringing back in his face, he hadn't
played games with women who hadn't known
what games they'd been playing. Only with
those who'd wanted what he had: pleasure and
nothing more.

But if this woman, this beautiful silver girl,
was someone who didn't understand what was
going on here, then he'd made another grave
error.

*You keep making them. One would almost
think that your father was right about you all
along. That you're unfit to rule—*

Galen cut that thought off before it could
form.

It was too late to put her out on the street,
not that he was crass enough to do that, but he
should definitely bring this little episode to a
close. Of course, he should never have dragged
her into his limo to start with, but, since he had,
the correct behaviour now would be to take her
back to his residence, give her some refresh-
ments if she wanted them, then get a car to return her to wherever she was staying.

He had to assume she'd been vetted and had

signed all the usual NDAs—she wouldn't have been at the club if she hadn't—but he'd get his security to double-check anyway. He had to be meticulous about any indiscretion. He couldn't afford to give his uncle any excuse to drag his past before the media and once again question his fitness to rule.

He became aware that she was watching him from beneath her lashes. 'Thank you,' he said, allowing some warmth in his tone. 'You were a pleasure. But now we'll be going to my residence, and from there I'll see you returned to your accommodation safely.'

She frowned. 'What do you mean I will be returned? I thought—'

'You thought what?' he interrupted, trying not to sound sharp because he didn't want to snap at her. 'Forgive me, but if you were expecting to stay, then I must disappoint you.'

'Why not? Didn't you like it?'

'I don't do one-night stands.' An edge had begun to creep into his voice no matter how he tried to stop it. 'At least not with those who don't know what they're getting themselves into.'

Her frown deepened, the sharp glitter of anger in her eyes. 'A one-night stand usually covers the entire night, not ten minutes in the back of a limo.'

Something inside him stirred, the young man

he'd once been, addicted to every adrenaline rush he could get his hands on, the more forbidden the better. Who'd loved a challenge, most especially when the one challenging him was a woman. And even though he'd told himself he wasn't going to do this, he moved over her once again, settling himself between her thighs and pressing her hands down on either side of her head. 'Taking that tone with me,' he murmured, 'will get you into all kinds of trouble.'

A shudder went through her, but there was no fear in her eyes. Only that glittering anger along with something…hotter.

Did she like this? Did she like being restrained by him?

'Perhaps I want trouble,' she said. 'Perhaps that's exactly what I'm looking for.' She shifted as if straining against his hold and his body pinning her to the seat. Yet her movements were languid, sensual, making it clear that she did not actually want to get away from him.

Desire kicked yet again, deep in his gut. He hadn't played this particular game for many years, mainly because when he'd ascended the throne, he'd cut away all his baser appetites as the weaknesses they were, trying to put some distance between himself and his past.

That doesn't mean they've gone away.

Of course, it didn't. If they had, he wouldn't

have had Leo and he certainly wouldn't be in this limo right now.

You must try harder.

Yes. He must.

'I don't think you want that,' he said. 'You'll be going back to wherever you come from tonight.'

Her chin came up, challenging him once again. 'What about you? What about what you want? Or are kings not allowed to have anything?'

'You shouldn't argue with me.' He tightened his grip on her wrists, settling more completely on her. 'I am the King of this country.'

'Of this country, yes, but I'm not from here, and you're not my king.'

Her pulse at the base of her throat had quickened and her voice was husky and breathless. She was aroused, he could smell it, and her need sparked his own, along with a dark kind of thrill that wound around him and pulled tight.

He did not want to let her go. He wanted to keep her here, beneath him, the whole night. He wanted to explore this desire, indulge himself completely, and, after all, he'd already had her once. What difference would it make if he kept her?

He was tired of constantly having to hold himself back. Tired of constantly checking himself and making sure nothing he did would cause his past to rear its ugly head. He hadn't had a woman in a year, and he missed it, and not just the sex but physical closeness too.

Surely, one night was allowed. No one would know. No one.

'Do you like to fight, silver girl?' he murmured, staring down into her dark eyes. 'Is that what you want? To fight me? Prove yourself against me?'

Heat flared in her eyes. 'You didn't answer my question. Why should I answer yours?'

Galen was conscious of a building excitement, because that look told him all he needed to know, as had that sharp response. Yes, she liked to fight, and she certainly wanted to fight him.

'Your question,' he said slowly. 'About what I want.' He flexed his hips, pressing the growing hardness behind his zip against the slick softness between her thighs and she shuddered, giving a little gasp. 'Kings are not allowed to have anything for themselves, it's true. But a man can have whatever he wants.'

Her gaze had gone smoky, once more drifting to his mouth. 'And what does this man want?'

'You know the answer to that already.' He shifted once more, making her gasp yet again. 'But I only have a night to give you. There can be nothing more. And afterwards, there will be documents for you to sign. My privacy is very important, and I expect you to honour it.'

'Yes.' Her voice was thick. 'Of course.'

He lowered his head, so he was inches away from her dark eyes, staring down into them, her luscious mouth almost but not quite touching his. 'Are you sure you want this? Because if you have a night with me, it will be *all* night. And we will not be sleeping. If you change your mind, do it now. I won't give you another chance.'

She said nothing, only stared back at him, and strangely, even though he'd always been able to read people like an open book, he had no idea what she was thinking. Then her hips moved once more, making his breath catch. And she shook his hands away, slid her fingers into his hair and brought his mouth down on hers.

CHAPTER THREE

Solace woke with a start, unsure for a couple of moments of where she was.

She seemed to be lying in a massive and very comfortable bed, surrounded by pillows, in a big room with white walls, and large white curtains drawn over the windows. Clearly it was morning since there was a line of bright gold painted along the dark wooden floor from the sunlight shining through a crack in the curtains.

The room was sparsely furnished with an antique chest of drawers thrust up against a wall, a long, low couch sitting beneath the windows and a brightly patterned silk rug on the floor.

It was very much *not* the cheap hostel she'd been staying in for the last couple of days.

Then she became aware of something else: not only was there was an arm circling her waist, a very muscular, heavy arm, but she was also naked.

She stared at the bright line of sunlight on

the floor as memories began to filter through, of where she was and who she was with, and what had happened the night before.

The nightclub, the limo, deep blue eyes staring into hers. His hands gripping her, his body pinning her, his mouth…

The king you surrendered to.

Solace swallowed and closed her eyes a moment. Oh, yes, she'd surrendered. She'd surrendered completely, giving herself up to him as if she'd been waiting all her life to do just that, lost in the way he held her in his strong hands. The power of him making her feel as if she could push against him as hard as she could, dash herself against him like a wave against a rock and he wouldn't budge. He wouldn't let her go. There was something comforting in that, something that made her feel safe. She didn't know why.

He was right. You did like fighting him.

She had. And she'd liked the surrender afterwards even more.

Heat washed over her, her entire body prickling at the memory, made even more intense by the hot press of his powerful body behind her.

Remember why you're here.

The thought turned the prickling heat into an icy wave and she had to catch breath.

Blackmail. That was why she was here. She

had to take pictures and blackmail the King into giving her son back. She'd forgotten about that the night before. He'd made her forget everything, even her own name, and when she'd finally fallen into an exhausted sleep, all she'd been conscious of was the feeling of being safe again. Of being protected.

A lie. She was never safe and there had never been anyone to protect her. Katherine had once told her that she'd love to be Solace's mum, and that Solace could live with her permanently, and Solace had believed her. But then Katherine had changed her mind and Solace been bounced to another home.

Never trust anyone, that was the lesson. Never trust what people told you. And most of all, never trust those feelings of safety, because they were lies too.

In the end, all you'd ever have was yourself. *In your case, you can't even trust that.*

Shame, sharp as barbed wire, wound around her heart, the line of gold on the floor blurring as her eyes prickled.

Fiercely, she forced the tears back.

She wouldn't be weak again, not as she'd been after the birth of her baby. She'd allowed fear and despair and the overwhelming guilt at what she'd done undermine her and it had taken her six months to pull herself out of the pit of postnatal depression she'd fallen into. She wasn't going to fall into it again. *Never.*

She'd never forget the three people who'd turned up on the doorstep of her grotty flat, literally the day after she'd had her son, either. She'd felt as if she were sitting at the bottom of a deep, dark well, with mile-high walls all around her, unable to get out. And those people, two men in black suits and a smiling woman in some kind of uniform, had seemed…kind.

The woman had explained who she was and that they were from Kalithera, and could they come inside because they needed to talk to her.

So, she'd let them in. And in her tiny bedsit, her baby screaming on the bed since she'd had no bassinet or baby things—he'd come a couple of days early and very unexpectedly—and no money to buy them anyway, the woman had told her that the man she'd been with nine months earlier at that ball was the King of Kalithera. And he wanted his son.

Shock and the fug of birth hormones still flooding her system had made her mute and slowed her thinking, so she'd just stared at the woman, her brain struggling to make sense of everything. She'd still been struggling to make sense of the fact that she'd had a baby at all, let alone the fact that her baby was a king's son.

Both she and the baby were to come to Kalithera, the woman had said kindly, and the King would take care of everything.

It had sounded so good. It had sounded perfect.

But no one took care of everything, she knew that for a fact, which must mean what the woman had told her was a lie. Not so much that her son was the son of a king—the uniforms, the black, expensive car in the street, the air of wealth and authority that clung to all three people made her sure of it—but that she was welcome. Because why? What would a king want with the likes of her? Yes, she was the mother of his child, but she was a poor nobody with no money and no education, and she knew what happened to poor nobodies. They were either taken advantage of or forgotten, especially by people in authority.

Her first impulse had been to refuse, to pick up her baby and hold him tight, send the people away. But then she'd looked around her tiny flat, at the mould on the ceilings and the peeling lino. The lack of a bassinet. The lack of anything resembling baby things because she'd only found out she was pregnant a week before she'd given birth. She'd had no money. No support. She'd known nothing about being a mother. She'd had nothing. What kind of life could she have given her child? He'd had no future with her, none at all.

It had been then that the dark pit had opened up beneath her feet and swallowed her whole.

She'd signed all the documents they'd given her, not seeing any of them, and when they'd told her there would be money in her account, she'd nodded blankly.

It was only after they'd finally gone and her flat had echoed with emptiness and absence, that the crushing weight of what she'd done had flattened her.

A wave of unexpected grief and guilt came, and she had to fight to force it back.

No, she couldn't let that overwhelm her. That was why she was here. She was here to fix the mistake she'd made, to get her baby back however she could.

Taking a calming breath, she gave the room a careful survey.

The night before, the limo had pulled up outside a house in a well-to-do part of the city. She hadn't been paying much attention, too occupied with Galen, and she hadn't paid attention when he'd pulled her out of the car and hurried her up the steps into the house either. Or when he'd carried her upstairs into this bedroom. And especially not when they'd finally ended up in this bed.

But her clothes must be around somewhere and hopefully her clutch, since her phone was in it.

Finally, she spotted a small pile of silver fabric near the door, which must be her dress. The stiletto sandals she'd been wearing lay not far away and in a piece of good luck, right near the bed, was her silver-mesh clutch.

Carefully, she glanced over her shoulder to check on the man behind her.

His face was relaxed in sleep, his breathing deep and even, and for a moment she just stared at him, part of her wondering how someone like her had managed to seduce a man like him. A king. A beautiful, powerful man, from one of the most ancient and aristocratic families in Europe, while she...

She was a nobody of unknown parentage, who'd dropped out of school, who stacked supermarket shelves and cleaned offices for a living. Not that there was anything wrong with that—she was proud of the fact that she earned her own money—but it was hardly at the same level as running an entire country.

She wasn't rich, she wasn't beautiful, and she had no power to speak of...

But no, that was being defeatist. She was changing things. She *would* change things. She was going back to school, and she'd apply herself and get great marks. Then she'd work hard and get into university and hopefully study law. And once she had her degree, she could use it to help people. People like herself.

How she'd do all of that with a child she had no idea, but she'd work it out. First, and most important of all, was getting that child back where he belonged. With her.

Solace slowly leaned over the side of the bed and reached for her clutch.

Behind her, Galen shifted, his arm tightening.

She froze, trying not to breathe. If he woke up now, it would ruin everything.

If only she'd done this last night, it would have been easier. She should have stayed awake until he'd gone to sleep and then taken some pictures. But she hadn't. She'd gone straight to sleep, lying warm and sated in his arms.

You were a fool.

Yes, and now she had to make up for it.

She waited until Galen's breathing had evened out, then reached for the clutch again. This time he didn't move so she was able to grab the bag and extract her phone. Typing in her code to unlock it, she pulled up the camera app and switched it to selfie mode.

It was a good phone, one she'd paid for with the blood money the Kalitherans had put into her account after she'd let them take her baby away. Because her old one was cheap, and the camera was terrible, and she'd needed a good camera if she was going to do this properly.

Putting her head back down on the pillow, she lifted the phone, holding it so Galen's face was clearly in the shot while hers was mostly out of it, leaving only her pale hair and a bare shoulder so people knew exactly what was going on here.

Taking pictures of him was wrong. It was a gross breach of his trust, of his privacy, and she didn't want to do it. She didn't want to blackmail him either.

But she'd exhausted every other avenue she could think of. She had to have her baby back, fix the terrible mistake she'd made in giving him up. Because while she might be a bad mother, she knew what it was like to grow up without one, and surely even a bad mother was better than none at all.

Maybe not. Maybe he's better off here. Maybe he's better off without you.

No, she didn't believe that. She couldn't.

Her hand shook as she fumbled for the button to take the picture, so the first shot was blurry, but through sheer force of will she steadied it and took a few more. Then she lowered the phone and shut her eyes, her heartbeat racing.

There, it was done. The photos would automatically go into her cloud storage, and she could access them anywhere from there. She already had a list of media organisations she knew would be more than happy to receive them.

But taking the pictures had been one of the easier parts of this mission. Now, she had to face the hardest part of all: blackmailing a king.

There was movement behind her, and she only had time to take a sharp, surprised breath before she was pulled over onto her back, her wrists taken in strong hands and pinned to the pillow on either side of her head. An extremely powerful male body shifted between her thighs, holding her down, and then she was looking up into a pair of furious blue eyes.

'What are you doing?' Galen demanded.

Ice flooded through her, freezing her solid.

His gaze went to the phone she had still clutched in her hand and back again. 'You took pictures.'

'I didn't, I—'

His head lowered, blue fire in his eyes, his voice low and very, very dangerous. 'Do. Not. Lie. To. Me.'

Fear wrapped icy claws around her throat and for a second all she could do was lie there, flattened by the force of his rage.

Remember what he did. He might be a king, but you are a mother, and he took your son from you.

True. She hadn't come all the way to Kali-thera, bribed her way into an exclusive club, and seduced a king only to cower before him like a kicked dog.

She'd come to take back what he'd stolen from her.

She *was* a mother and, while she might not have the first idea how to be one, she certainly knew how to fight and so she'd fight for her son.

Clinging to that thought, Solace forced away the fear and steeled herself, reaching for her own anger as she stared straight back into Galen's burning blue eyes.

'Yes,' she said coldly. 'I took some pictures. Of you and I.'

His hands on her wrists tightened, his grip just on the edge of pain. 'Why?'

She swallowed, her mouth dry, her heartbeat like a drum in her head. But when she spoke, her voice was steady. 'To blackmail you with, of course.'

There was no point pretending any more, and in a way it was a relief that finally the moment was here. In fact, she was almost proud of herself. She'd come a long way in six months and her plan had ended up being wildly successful, and soon the awful mistake she'd made would be fixed.

The look on Galen's face was terrible. 'Black-mail me for what? Money? Power?'

'No.' Solace held tight to her own rage. The rage that had dragged her out of that pit and put her feet on the path that had led here. 'I couldn't care less about money or power. What I want, Galen Kouros, is my son.'

Galen heard the words, but they didn't mean anything to him. He was so angry he could barely think. Some of his anger was for her, that she thought she could blackmail *him*, but most of it was reserved for himself and his own monumental stupidity.

He'd allowed his groin to do his thinking for him the night before, and he hadn't done any of the things he should have, such as waited for his security staff to a) do a background check and b) search her person for anything that could be a security risk, such as phones.

But no, he'd decided he was going to allow himself a night of no restraint and so he'd rushed her from the limo straight into his bedroom, no thought in his head but to have her naked beneath him as quickly as possible.

When will you learn? Ten years a king and you still haven't mastered yourself. Alexandros was right about you.

Perhaps. Certainly Leo existed because he

hadn't mastered himself, and, while he'd never regret his son, Leo's existence had also complicated his life to an impossible extent.

Now he'd complicated it even further.

'Your son?' he snapped, fury burning in his veins like wildfire. 'What are you talking about?'

She seemed very calm for a woman in the process of blackmailing him. 'You don't recognise me, do you?'

The familiarity that had tugged at him, their chemistry, the sounds she'd made as he'd pushed inside her... He remembered those sounds. They'd haunted his dreams for over an entire year. They'd haunted him last night, in this very bed, while he'd touched and tasted every inch of her curvy little body.

She was warm beneath him, but he could feel the tension in her, could see it too in the line of her stubborn jaw. Her gaze was dark, and she didn't look away this time, not the way she had the night before.

He let go of her hands and smoothed back her silky pale hair, flattening it tight to her skull. She made no move to stop him, her eyes glittering with defiance.

He stared, studying the lines of her face. It was difficult to tell without the mask, but... No, it couldn't be her. She'd had grey eyes.

'Who are you?' he demanded, the fury in him burning hotter, higher. 'Tell me.'

'You already know who I am.' Her voice was flat, yet he could hear the edge of anger in it.

It's her, you know it is. You knew it the moment you saw her.

Cold washed over him, freezing his anger, chasing away the last remains of the pleasant warmth and satiation he'd woken up with. Before he'd become aware of her lowering her hand and wondered why she was holding a phone.

Before it had penetrated that there could be only one reason.

It was her, it had to be. The woman he'd met at the masquerade ball.

He searched her face, still holding her hair back, and sure enough, there was the line of her lower lip that he hadn't been able to stop himself from licking and nipping, so full and soft. And her eyes looking up into his, full of defiance now, but last night they'd been full of desire. Full of want.

Just beyond the edge of her iris he could see a faint line. Contacts.

His rage leapt, but, with a massive effort of will, he forced it away. If this morning had taught him anything at all, it was that he could not afford to indulge in *any* of his weaknesses. He wasn't a child throwing a tantrum as he had been during his time at Oxford. These last ten years he'd learned how to behave like a king and now he was one. Down to his bones.

Galen let her go and shoved back the sheets, getting out of bed and striding over to where his clothes lay in a heap by the door. He began to dress, pulling on his underwear and then his trousers.

'You will delete the photos,' he ordered as he zipped up his fly. 'And then you will answer every single one of my questions.'

She sat up, wrapping a sheet around her lush curves, her silky white-blonde hair falling around her shoulders. 'It's too late. They're in the cloud. It'll only take me a minute to put them up on social media.'

He couldn't tear his gaze from her pale skin, his body already hardening at the sight of her, but he forced the hunger away. It had no place here. It was sex that had led him into this situation, the physical chemistry that had exploded between them, and he would not let it master him again.

He stared at her coldly, going back over what she'd said now he'd had a chance to fully processes what was happening.

Her son. She'd said that was what she wanted when he'd asked. Not money, not power. Her son.

His son. *His*. Because she'd given him up.

She'd signed away her rights and had taken the money he'd authorised his representatives to give her should she not want to come to Kalithera. He'd tried to keep tabs on her subsequently, because his son should know who his mother was, but then she'd vanished without a trace. And Galen had let her, assuming she hadn't wanted Leo anyway.

Yet now, here she was, in his bed, blackmailing him.

Last night was never about you...

Something a lot like disappointment twisted in his chest, but he ignored it.

He could treat last night as yet another reminder of how unsuited he was to the crown he wore, or he could treat it as a warning. He couldn't afford more mistakes, not with Kostas still waiting for an opportunity to take Kalithera from him. And now Galen had not only a country to protect, but a succession to guard. Destroying his son's legacy and putting Kalithera at risk for the sake of his own lusts was inconceivable.

'You cannot possibly think,' he said icily, 'that I'd give my son away just because I didn't want a couple of pictures of myself in bed with you in the media?'

She was already very pale, now she went even paler. But her chin remained at a stubborn angle and still she didn't look away. 'Perhaps you might think differently when the media comes to camp on your doorstep,' she said. 'I don't imagine your reputation will last long after that.'

Deep inside him, past his fury, Galen was aware of another emotion, a reluctant, grudging respect he didn't want to acknowledge. After he'd had the news that she'd had his child, he'd read the file his staff had given him about her. He knew she'd grown up in the foster system and that she hadn't finished her schooling. That she did various low-paid jobs to make ends meet and that her current living situation was not ideal for her, let alone for a baby.

Remembering her grey eyes and wild passion the night of the ball, he'd felt sorry for her and had very much wanted her to come to Kalithera with their son. But his aides had told him she'd refused, no reason given.

He'd been furious about that, furious she'd given up their child without protest, only to disappear off the face of the earth, and he'd assumed all sorts of things about the kind of woman who'd give up her child for money. And he didn't know why she was back to claim Leo now, but one thing was clear: she was a fighter.

Still, if she thought blackmail would work on him then she needed to think again. She'd get no more money from him, if that was what she was after.

'Then your imagination is sadly lacking.' He folded his arms across his bare chest. 'I have the best PR team in the business, and they can spin anything.' It was no less than the truth.

'Oh?' Her cheeks were now flushed, the glitter of anger in her eyes becoming more pronounced. 'You mean like how they spun your son's mother dying tragically in childbirth? Or rather your *fiancée*. Since apparently you were going to marry her after a whirlwind secret romance.' Her tone dripped with disdain.

Galen had never thought he'd be in the position of having to justify the story his PR team had come up with to explain Leo's existence. That had painted him in the light of a grieving single father who'd lost his love tragically.

He hadn't liked the lie, but it had been necessary to stop Kostas from digging too deeply in places he shouldn't and bringing it up with the media.

His team, of course, didn't know the exact reason why it was so important that not a breath of scandal be attached to his name. All they knew was that the reputation of the King had to be protected and so protect it they had.

No one had expected Leo's actual mother—

the mother who'd given him up—to turn up in Kalithera to get her son back.

Yet here she was and now he had to deal with it.

'I'm not explaining the decisions of my PR team to you,' he said coldly, ignoring the faint sting of what could not possibly be shame. 'The fact remains that blackmail will not work on me and so you have nothing.'

There were dark circles beneath her eyes, and, through his anger and the cold grip of control, he was conscious of a certain protectiveness.

He'd felt it that night over a year ago, in the deserted office. In the aftermath of passion, he'd held her against the wall with his body, both of them panting, and looked down into her face. There had been wonder in her expression, and desire and not a little awe, and protectiveness had swept through him. She had been a stranger, he hadn't even known her name, yet she'd held nothing back. She'd given herself to him so passionately it was as if those moments with him had been her first taste of pleasure.

Yet then she'd ripped herself away from him and run, vanishing into the crowds before he'd had a chance to talk with her. He hadn't been able to go after her since he'd been the guest of honour, and afterwards he'd been inundated with all the formalities of an official visit.

You knew she was a virgin. You knew. And you left her alone and pregnant with your child.

Guilt caught at him, along with another sting of shame, but again, he forced them away. He hadn't known she was pregnant, not until his security team had finally managed to track her down, following up as a matter of course since they monitored anyone he had an interaction with. As to the virginity, he hadn't known that either, not when they'd barely exchanged a handful of sentences.

'You think I'm bluffing?' she said shakily. 'I'm not.'

'Nor am I.' He met her gaze, held it. 'Go on. Do it. Upload them. My team won't break a sweat explaining them. Though if you are indeed who you say you are, it still won't get you your son.'

She'd gone pale as ashes now, her dark eyes full of accusation and anger. Yet she didn't move for the phone. 'You took my baby from me,' she said instead. 'You took him away. And I want him back. Now.'

He should bring this little scene to a close, that would be the safest thing. He should call his security, get them to delete the photos, and then send her back to London where she came from. Perhaps he'd even send her first class or on one of his private jets—there was no need for jail or anything too heavy-handed. She hadn't actually done anything, after all.

Except…there was a desperate but determined note in her voice that tugged at him. She wanted her baby—their baby—and that fierce look in her eyes didn't seem feigned. His team had told him she'd signed those papers willingly, yet…that didn't gel with the pale woman sitting in his bed. Who'd presumably come all the way from London to seduce him and then blackmail him, purely to get her baby back.

'What do you mean I took him?' he demanded. '*You* didn't want him. You signed all those documents and you—' He broke off as she abruptly shoved herself off the bed and stormed over to where he stood, the white sheet still wrapped around her trailing in her wake.

She stopped in front of him, her dark gaze fierce. 'I *did* want him. But when those…people arrived at my flat, it was the day after I'd given birth and I was shell-shocked. I couldn't take in what they were saying, then they…they said I could come to Kalithera too, but I… I thought it was a lie, so I refused. Then they gave me some documents, and I signed them, but only so my son would be safe. But I didn't want to give him up, I *didn't*.' Her whole body was trembling, her eyes glittering. She looked as if she were preparing to throw herself in front of a truck. 'Why did you take him?' She took another step, their bodies nearly touching. *'Why?'*

He did not know this woman. He'd never known her. Yet he'd spent a year thinking about their one encounter, and last night he'd spent hours enjoying the gift of her body, hours giving her pleasure and letting her give the same to him.

He had no reason to believe what she was saying but…

She hadn't faked any of the orgasms he'd given her, he'd stake his life on that. Her pleasure had been real, and this fury and the pain he could see beneath it…they were real too.

You took her child away from her.

The sting of shame became a thorn, piercing him, along with a guilt that cut even deeper. He knew that fear and anguish himself, had experienced both the moment he'd discovered Leo's existence.

You thought it was only money she was after. But she didn't want to give him up. You should have tried harder to find her. You should have tried harder, full stop.

Oh, he knew. He knew very well how much harder he should have tried. It applied to everything he did, and yet it seemed no matter how hard he tried, it wasn't enough. It would never be enough.

How many more mistakes will you make? Are you sure Kostas wouldn't be a better king?

No, he couldn't think that. He wouldn't. Kalithera *was* better off with him on the throne and, besides, he had to deal with what was happening in the present, not his own insidious doubts.

However, there was too much anger in the room and they both needed a bit of time and space to compose themselves. Certainly, he did.

He stayed still, arms folded, staring down at her. 'We need to talk.'

'I don't want to talk. I want to —'

'You're white as that sheet. You're tired. And you're naked. I think you'd feel better after you've had a shower, got dressed and had some breakfast.'

Her gaze flashed and her mouth opened, no doubt to keep on arguing with him, but he went on before she could. 'Besides, I need to ascertain you are who you say you are and various other things.' Her mouth opened yet again, but again he went on. 'Or would you be happy talking to a complete stranger about the private details of your baby?'

She gave him a furious look. 'You don't need to be so condescending. I'm not a child.'

'I am well aware of that, believe me.' He

raised a brow. 'Unless you'd like to discuss our son while you're stark naked and still smelling of sex and me?'

She flushed, yet her stubborn little chin remained lifted.

Good. Anger suited her. He liked that she wasn't so pale and had stopped trembling. Perhaps he should keep her angry. It was better than her fear and anguish. Those he didn't like, not at all.

'You really don't care about those photos?' She was still looking at him defiantly.

'No,' he said with absolute truth. 'But I can't imagine why you'd want to resort to taking pictures of me when a simple phone call would have sufficed.'

'You think I didn't try?' she shot back. 'I didn't actually want to blackmail you, believe it or not, but every call I made to the Kalitheran embassy in London, every email I sent, they all thought I was lying. I even went in there myself, but then they called Security and threw me out.' The acid in her tone bit deeper. 'Apparently when you're a poor nobody, no one believes you when you tell them that you've had their king's child.'

He could well imagine. His reputation was so rock solid that the very idea some strange Englishwoman would have had a night with him and borne his child would have been laughable.

But a nobody? She was hardly that, not having come all the way from England to Kalithera to blackmail him *and* almost succeeding. Naive perhaps, and obviously scrappy and determined. But very much *not* a nobody.

He eyed her, lingering on her silky, pale hair and how it flowed over her shoulders, then further, where her hands gripped the sheet. He'd only have to tug gently, and it would come away, leaving her naked…

Predictably, his body hardened, and he could tell by the way she flushed that she'd picked up on his thoughts. Her fingers tightened on her sheet even as her gaze drifted down over his chest and her luscious mouth opened slightly.

The familiar electricity of their chemistry began to build again, sparks arcing between them, and it took effort to push it away this time, but he managed.

He wouldn't compound the errors he'd made last night by taking her again. Not that it would have been appropriate anyway. She was still distressed and, besides, they had more important things to discuss.

'A nobody? Don't be ridiculous,' he said flatly, crushing the desire flooding through his veins. 'I'll have food brought to you and perhaps more suitable clothes. We'll talk in half an hour.'

Then before he could change his mind, cross the space between them and rip the sheet from her hands, he turned on his heel and went out.

CHAPTER FOUR

SOLACE STARED AT the closed door, her knees weak. She'd stopped physically shaking, but she was trembling still, deep inside. And perhaps some of it was fear, but it wasn't all. Anger made up a good proportion, as did the nagging desire that had licked up the moment Galen's blue gaze had fallen to her shoulders and then to her hand where she still gripped her sheet.

Despite everything, despite the fear and the anger, she was conscious that he was standing very close and wearing only his trousers. His chest was bare and she could see every hard, carved muscle, and all she could think about was how she'd traced those muscles with her fingers the night before, and then with her tongue. His skin had tasted salty and delicious and had felt like velvet...

No. She couldn't be thinking about that, not any of it, not when her plan now lay in ruins.

She swallowed, bitter disappointment turning over inside her, tears stinging her eyes. God, would they ever stop? She was so tired of crying, so tired of fighting. So tired of nothing going right for her, no matter how hard she tried.

But being tired wasn't going to help and neither was crying about it. She'd been naive to think a couple of compromising pictures would be all she'd need to get her child back. Stupid even. Of course, a king would have an entire PR department dedicated to keeping his reputation clean, especially a king like him. After all, she probably wasn't the first woman to try this with him and she probably wouldn't be the last.

Solace turned and went over to the bed, sitting down on it and lacing her fingers together, clenching them hard. Taking a few deep breaths, she tried to calm herself so she could think.

The blackmail hadn't worked and castigating herself over her naivety wasn't going to get her any closer to her son. What she needed was to formulate another plan. The good thing was that now she actually had access to her son's father, so she wasn't starting from zero again. She was here, in his house, and he'd said they would talk.

Perhaps he wouldn't throw her in jail for her blackmail attempt. He'd certainly been furious enough about it, and the really stupid thing was, she understood why. She would have been too. The other stupid thing was—and she hated to admit this to herself—that part of her couldn't help but respect him for not caving instantly to her demands the way she'd hoped. He'd called her bluff and she'd been fully prepared to grab her phone and do what she'd threatened, but she could see the steel in his eyes. He wasn't going to hand over their child for the sake of a couple of pictures, and that very same part of her, the fierce mother instinct, couldn't help but admire him for it.

He's a king. You really thought he'd give in so easily?

She had, but as she'd already thought, she'd been naive. Not that there was any point going over it again. She had to figure out what she was going to do now.

Half an hour, he'd said, then they'd talk. Which would give her time to have that shower, get dressed and eat something. Because while she hated being told what to do, he hadn't been wrong. Having a conversation about their son while she was pretty much naked apart from a sheet made her uncomfortable. And she did *not* smell of sex and him. Did she?

Well, even if she did she wasn't going to for much longer.

Slipping off the bed, she headed determinedly into the en-suite bathroom. It was huge, with a big, white-tiled walk-in shower and a multitude of jets, plus a vanity of long white marble veined with gold. A bath made from the same material stood near big windows that looked out onto the green of a private garden.

It took her aback, the sight of so much luxury. She'd never seen anything like it.

Her little bedsit had enough room for a sofa bed and nothing else, and she'd thought *that* luxurious after some of the foster homes she'd been in, mainly because it was hers and she didn't have to share it with anyone.

But this…

Your child is heir to all this. Would you seriously take him away from it?

The thought hurt. Because while she was in a much better place than the black hole she'd been in six months ago, nothing she had equalled this. Here he would be a prince, heir to a kingdom, while with her…

He'll be a nobody just like you.

Solace shoved that thought away. She might be a nobody, but a child needed its mother. She'd never had one herself, never had any kind of family, and the lack had been a wound she'd carried with her all her life. It wasn't something she wanted for her son.

But he does have a family. He has his father.

Okay, it was time to stop thinking about that. She went over to the shower and spent a couple of moments trying to figure out how it worked before dropping the sheet and stepping under the fall of water.

It was glorious. She stood there with her eyes closed, enjoying the warmth, letting the water stream over her and wash away the fear and stress of the past quarter of an hour. She couldn't give in to it; being afraid wouldn't get her son back.

Opening her eyes, she began to wash herself, noticing as she did so small bruises and red patches marring her skin. Galen had left marks.

A wave of heat that had nothing to do with the shower swept over her and she groaned softly, lifting her hands to her face and trying to shove the memories from her head. Thinking about the night before wouldn't help either. She had to formulate a new plan, but what?

How was she going to get her child back? *Could* she even get her child back? He'd given her a glimpse of the steel inside him. He wouldn't give their son to her, no matter what she did. Oh, she could try and manipulate him by playing the mother card and perhaps using their son's future feelings as a weapon against him, but that felt wrong. She didn't want to use their son as a pawn when the battle was between her and Galen. That was selfish.

Taking him away from his father is selfish.

Solace gritted her teeth. Okay, she'd allow that it cut both ways. Taking her child from Galen would leave Galen feeling as she did now, as if there was a hole in her soul, and she wouldn't wish that on him. But then where did that leave her?

If she couldn't take her child back to England, what else could she do? She couldn't stay indefinitely in Kalithera, not on a tourist visa, and even if she could, would Galen allow her access to her baby? Given the statement his PR department had issued about the fate of his son's mother—presumably to protect his spotless reputation—she could now never be acknowledged as the mother of his child. And she suspected that even if access was granted, it would be limited.

Solace dropped her hands from her face and stared hard at the white tiles in front of her, thinking.

Perhaps she needed to offer Galen something. She had no skills, no useful work experience except stacking supermarket shelves and serving people food, and her education was only of the most basic kind. The only useful thing she had was her body and that, at least, she knew he wanted. Perhaps she could offer to be his mistress? Or maybe, if that wasn't acceptable, she could be her son's nanny? He'd already have one, but maybe Galen would be okay with her helping in some small way.

It felt like begging for something she was already entitled to, and she hated that thought, but she couldn't see any other choice. She had no power here except that which Galen chose to give her, and the only alternative was giving up and going home, and she couldn't do that either.

She couldn't let her own pride get in the way. After all, her feelings didn't matter, only her child did. Perhaps being honest with Galen was the key. Perhaps she'd give him the brutal truth of why she'd signed away her rights as a parent, why she'd given up their son to him. Tell him about the postnatal depression, about her reasons for resorting to blackmail, and about how giving away her baby had torn a hole clean through her heart.

He was a fair man, that was what they said about him as a king. Surely, he'd listen. Surely, he'd give her something.

It went against all her instincts to bare her soul to anyone at all, let alone a man and most especially a man with such power, but what other option did she have?

She would do anything for her son. Anything at all.

Strangely, the decision made her feel stronger than she had for months, a new kind of determination flowing through her. She'd do what she had to for her son's sake and maybe Galen would acknowledge that, maybe he wouldn't, but she'd have tried.

You think that makes up for what you did? You gave him away as your mother gave you away. What makes you any better?

But she shut that thought away as she dried herself off and wrapped herself in a towel.

When she came out of the bathroom, she saw that a small table had been set up in the middle of the room, with plates of toast and eggs and bacon. There were pots of jam and honey, and a slab of creamy butter. A coffee pot steamed gently, filling the room with the scent of fresh coffee.

Solace's stomach rumbled, reminding her that she hadn't eaten since her hurried dinner the night before and she was starving.

Galen's pronouncements about eating and getting dressed irritated her all over again, but while she might be uneducated, she was not stupid, so she put away her irritation, got herself a plate of food and some coffee, and had breakfast.

Annoyingly, she felt better after that and, even more annoying, she liked the dress that had been laid out for her on the bed while she'd been in the shower. It was a simple tiered sundress of thick white cotton that tied at her shoulders, and looked loose and comfortable and casual, as well as pretty.

She liked pretty things yet never had the money to buy them, and she'd have loved the dress if it hadn't obviously been something he wanted her to wear.

Then again, who cared? She liked it and she didn't want to wear the mesh dress again. It felt wrong to wear something so exposing when she was going to discuss her child's future.

Perhaps you should. He might like you on your knees. After all, what else do you have to offer?

Solace's jaw hardened. No, she'd offered her body once and he'd taken it. But she wouldn't do it again. No more manipulation. She'd try honesty and see where that got her.

It won't get you anywhere. It never has before. And would he even believe you anyway?

But Solace ignored the thought, picking up the pretty white dress and going about making herself presentable.

Ten minutes later, a knock came on the bedroom door.

She took a breath, steadied herself, and then went to answer it.

A man in the blue and silver palace uniform

stood on the other side. 'His Majesty will see you now. Please, follow me.'

Solace stepped out of the bedroom and followed the man dutifully.

She remembered the hall from the night before, though Galen had been carrying her at the time, and she hadn't really taken a good look around. They'd both been far more interested in getting to the bedroom.

It was a wide hallway with a polished wooden floor covered by a thick silk runner. The walls were white and hung with various paintings, some abstracts with lots of colour and some more monochrome. The ceilings were high, and windows at the end of the hall let in light.

The stairs were of some dark wood, and swept down to a small but high-ceilinged entranceway. It wasn't as grand as she'd expected from a king's residence, but she rather liked that. It felt more like a home than a palace did, and she liked the spare furnishings too. Nothing was ostentatious or overblown. Just quietly luxurious.

The staff member led her down another hallway to a door that he opened and ushered her through into the room beyond.

It seemed to be a study. Heavy wooden bookcases lined the walls closest to the door, while on the opposite side of the room big windows looked out onto an atrium-style garden, with a square colonnade with white columns around it and a fountain with a lush garden around it in the middle. Also in the room was an enormous antique oak desk with an equally enormous portrait of a man on the wall behind it.

The room was empty.

The man indicated the chair standing before the desk. 'Please sit. His Majesty will be with you shortly.'

He withdrew, shutting the door behind him and leaving her in silence.

Solace sat, her hands clenched in her lap, and stared at the portrait behind the desk.

It was in oils, of a man standing behind a table. He was very tall, his hair more white than black, and wearing formal black clothing. There were medals on his chest and on the table was a crown. He was a handsome man, though unsmiling, fierce dark eyes looked out at the viewer in what Solace couldn't help thinking was a slightly judgmental fashion.

She didn't recognise the man, but the crown gave a hint.

It must be Alexandros Kouros, Galen's father.

There wasn't much resemblance in his face that Solace could see, but the fierce quality of that stare was unmistakable.

Suddenly the office door opened, and Galen came in and all the air in the room disappeared.

He'd changed into a fresh pair of dark grey trousers and a deep blue business shirt that accentuated the colour of his eyes. His hair was damp as if he'd freshly showered and it was clear he'd shaved.

He was absolutely devastating.

Galen strode to the desk and stood behind it, and for long moments he didn't speak, his gaze sweeping over her, his expression impenetrable, every inch of him a king.

'So,' he said at last. 'You will give me an explanation for why you changed your mind about our son, Solace Ashworth, and you will give it to me now.'

Half an hour. That was all it had been. Half an hour since he'd last seen her, after spending all night with her, and yet the moment her gaze met his, he felt the same gut punch of need that he'd felt the night before.

Except this time her eyes weren't dark but the sharp, piercing grey that had haunted his dreams for so long, a crystalline colour like frost on a winter pond. The effect of that gaze was the same too, a sword right through his heart.

She sat on the chair in front of his desk, wearing the dress he'd had one of his staff members do a last-minute dash for—a pretty white thing that made her look pale and lovely—and all he wanted to do was to rip it off her.

It was galling that, even after the night before, the desire for her still dogged him. However, at least he was now in control of it. He wasn't going to let it become a problem, not again.

Conscious of Alexandros's gaze watching from the wall behind him, Galen folded his arms and waited. While he'd showered and changed, his staff had been busy confirming her identity and updating the file they already had on her. And by the time he'd finished buttoning his shirt, that file was in his hands, and he'd familiarised himself with it.

She'd indeed had a difficult life. The kind of life that might have crushed another person, yet it had not crushed her.

She sat in the chair bolt upright, hair lying in waves over her white shoulders, her chin lifted, her stare very, very sharp. The epitome of uncrushed and determinedly so.

It made him even more curious as to what had changed her mind after giving Leo away and why she was here now, six months later, prepared to blackmail him to get Leo back.

'I didn't change my mind.' Anger coloured

her voice, he heard it loud and clear. 'I *never* wanted to give up *my* son, I told you that.'

'Yet you did.' He decided to let the 'my son' go for the meantime. 'I've seen the documents. It's your signature on every one of them. You said something about wanting him to be safe?'

Her mouth tightened, small silver sparks glittering in her eyes. 'Okay, you want the story? I'll give you the story. I didn't know I was pregnant. I found out literally a week before he arrived and when he did, he was a couple of days early. I was in shock. My last pay cheque hadn't gone through yet and so I had no money to buy him anything. I was discharged from hospital hours after having him, and I had no support when I got home. I had no idea what to do.'

The silver sparks in her eyes were now flames. 'Your staff arrived the next day. And they told me who you were and whose baby I'd just had. And while I was still trying to get my head around that, they said I had to come to Kalithera with them because my son's father wanted him.' Her jaw line was rigid, her sharp gaze not leaving his. 'I...couldn't think properly. It was like my head was full of cotton wool and I couldn't understand why I was even being asked to come. I...didn't believe them that I'd be welcome. I didn't trust them. But I also knew he couldn't stay with me. He was heir to a kingdom and one day he'd sit on a throne, and I wanted that for him. Because he'd have nothing if he stayed with me. A life of poverty, growing up on council estates, and drugs and who knows what else?'

Her hands were clasped tightly in her lap, her knuckles white. 'I was so tired, so exhausted and all I could think about was how much safer he'd be with them, and so, yes, I gave him up. I gave him up so he could have a better life, and I regretted that decision the moment I made it. I'll regret it for the rest of my life.'

Galen didn't let his shock show. He hadn't known, not any of this. He'd been very clear with his staff about how they were to go about retrieving Leo. They were to do it sensitively and Solace was to accompany them, because he wasn't a monster. He wasn't going to rip away a child from its mother. Yet then they'd told him that she hadn't wanted to come and had given Leo up without protest, and he'd taken that at face value.

You keep making mistake after mistake. You should have gone yourself.

He should have, but he hadn't. Everything about getting Leo had had to be discreet. He couldn't have risked being seen in some down-at-heel street in London, not when the British press were so ruthless. The risk of discovery had been too great. Kostas would have been even more suspicious if Galen had disappeared only to return with a child, and even when the story had come out, he'd asked some difficult questions.

'My staff were under strict instructions,' he said. 'They weren't to coerce you in any way, and they were also to ensure that you'd feel welcome coming to Kalithera.'

'Oh, they explained. They were very clear. But like I said, I was in shock. I couldn't think and they were...impatient.'

Yes, they probably had been. He'd told them not to linger.

'We tried to contact you,' he said, because he had. 'But your phone number was disconnected, and your flat was empty. We had no way of finding out where you were. And I assumed...' He wasn't proud of this, he wasn't proud at all, but she deserved his honesty in return for her own. 'I assumed you'd taken the money and fled.'

Twin spots of brilliant colour burned in her pale cheeks. It was clear whatever confession she was going to make to him, it was going to cost her. 'No, I didn't. My phone died and I couldn't afford another, and I couldn't afford to stay in my flat either. I had postnatal depression and couldn't work.'

Yet more shock hit him. 'But the money—'

'You think I'd ever touch that money?' There was ferocity in her gaze now, a burning fury. 'No. That was blood money, and I didn't want a penny of it.'

You have made a complete and utter mess of this. As expected.

Galen had always hated the strict rules his father had imposed on him as a boy, rules that, no matter how hard he tried, seemed to have been set up precisely so he could fail them. To be good, obey his tutors, be polite and pleasant. Never allow his emotions or his own personal wants and needs to rule him.

Simple rules and yet always there had been something he did that was wrong. He'd laughed when he shouldn't, used the wrong title, run when he should have walked... Small things that his father had treated as huge failures. In the end he'd decided that there was no point in trying when nothing he did was right anyway, and so he'd let his anger at his father consume him.

Then Alexandros had died, and, to protect his country, Galen had had to take the throne, a throne that might not be his. And he'd found himself having to try yet again, to overcome the reputation he'd earned in England, to be the perfect King so no one would ever question his claim. And he'd thought, after ten years of solid rule, that finally he'd laid the ghost of his father to rest. That he might even deserve the throne he sat on...

But you don't, do you?

The thought sat in his head, searing him. In the space of a little over a year, not only had he compromised the integrity of his crown, he'd torn his son from his mother and left her with nothing. She had been done a terrible wrong and he was the cause, and, while her blackmail attempt had also been wrong, he knew what lengths a parent would go to for their child. He couldn't hold that against her.

His own guilt at his role in this was a knife blade. He had to make this right somehow. Yet at the same time, he couldn't put at risk the secret he had to keep.

She couldn't be acknowledged as Leo's mother, not given the story that had already been disseminated about how she'd died in childbirth. If it was found out that, not only was she alive, but also that the palace had lied, well... That would be an opportunity his uncle wouldn't let sit. Kostas would parade the decade-old scandal of that party in London Galen been discovered at, evidence that Galen hadn't been a fit choice of heir. Then he'd no doubt stir up trouble with the old rumours about Galen's mother and the affair she was reputed to have had, causing questions about Galen's parentage and whether he was indeed Alexandros's son...

No, he couldn't allow that, not for his country's sake and not for Leo's.

Uncrossing his arms, he put his hands on the edge of the desk, leaning on them. 'Then what is it that you want, Solace? I apologise for the way you've been treated. None of what happened to you was my intention, and I'll do everything I can to make it up to you. However...' He paused, because on this he would not be moved, no matter what she said. 'I'll not allow my son to be taken out of Kalithera. He is my heir therefore he stays with me, understand?'

'Yes, I understand.' Her back was very straight, and she didn't look away. 'Then I'll stay here with him.'

'And how do you envisage that working? You cannot be acknowledged as his mother, not since everyone thinks his mother is dead.'

'That's not my problem.' There was steel in her voice. '*You* took my baby away. *You* told the world his mother was dead. I had no choice in any of this, which makes it your issue to deal with, not mine.'

Galen was conscious of that heat building inside him again, the competitor responding to the challenge she'd just laid down, and it was a challenge, whether she knew it or not.

She might have seemed fragile and pale sitting there in her virginal white dress, but her silver eyes were hard and there was nothing but defiance in the tilt of her chin.

A proud, regal woman. A woman who'd been fighting for everything her entire life and now she was fighting for this, for her child.

Their child.

He couldn't imagine the childhood she'd had, with no stability anywhere, not even in her bloodline. It was the opposite of his, where he'd been told from birth who he was and who he'd eventually be. Yet he wasn't a stranger to instability, not when he didn't even know if the throne he sat on was truly his, or even if Alexandros was actually his father.

Not that he could tell a soul about that. It was his secret to bear.

Anyway, what was important now was deciding what to do with her, not getting curious about her, and the simplest thing would be to have her flown back to London and out of his hair. Yet…

He couldn't bring himself to do it. Sending her away would hurt her and he'd already hurt her enough as it was. The right thing to do

would be to find a way for her to stay in Kalithera and allow her access to Leo.

*Are you sure keeping her here is the right
thing to do, though? You know how weak you
can be.*

Yes, yes, he knew that. But he had himself
well in hand. She might have got under his skin
twice already, but there wouldn't be a third time.

Galen pushed himself up from his desk and
straightened. 'Naturally, it is my problem. I am
King here and I will decide how best to pro-
ceed.'

Her gaze was steely. 'If you send me home,
I'll fight you. I'm not going anywhere without
my son.'

This little warrior was quite a change from
the seductive, passionate woman of the night
before, and, he had to admit, it intrigued him.
He'd seen flashes of this same steel in the back
of his limo the night before and it had been...
sexy. Especially in combination with her white-
hot desire and the way she'd surrendered to him.

An intoxicating combination in a woman, if
he was honest with himself, and one he'd never
experienced before, not even back in his bad old
days of university.

*If you married her, it would solve all your
problems at once.*

The thought came out of nowhere and was so

ridiculous, he almost laughed. Because while it was true, he'd been thinking of a wife, he couldn't marry Solace. The Kings of Kalithera married women from important, aristocratic families, not poor commoners. He couldn't break tradition, not given how carefully Kostas watched him, and besides, given the mistakes he'd already made concerning Solace, marrying her would no doubt be a disaster. No, it wouldn't work.

He was going to have to think of something else.

'That won't be necessary,' he said. 'Though I'm not sure exactly how you think you can fight me.'

It was a pointless thing to add, and he wasn't sure why he had, especially when her gaze sparked and she virtually quivered in her seat with suppressed anger. As if she was a hair's breadth away from springing over his desk and strangling him.

'I may look powerless, but I'm not,' she said fiercely. 'I can create trouble for you.'

'You've already created trouble for me.'

'No, *you* created the trouble.' She paused, then spat, 'Your Majesty.'

You need to stop this. Baiting her is a terrible idea.

Especially when the gulf in their stations was

so vast. And most especially when he knew all too well that he was only doing it because he found her rage intoxicating. She was like a cornered alley cat, hissing and spitting because she had nowhere else to go, and was no doubt secretly terrified. In fact, him deliberately baiting her was not only cruel, it was also selfish.

So he ignored her sharp retort and looked into her bright silver eyes. 'Would you like to see him?' he asked.

CHAPTER FIVE

SOLACE HAD FELT as if she were going to spontaneously combust with rage. He was so cool and in command standing behind his desk, radiating authority. His voice sounded as icy as his blue eyes, as if nothing at all touched him. So very much not the man she'd been in bed with the night before.

She didn't know what to do.

She wanted to be as cool as he was, as in command and powerful, but all that honesty, laying out all the facts of what had happened to her, had ripped away her defences, leaving her feeling raw and exposed. She wasn't a man, and she certainly wasn't a king, and all she had was her anger, so that was what she'd grabbed hold of. The fire inside her that had propelled her out of the pit of depression and landed her here, in his study, telling a king she was going to fight him.

She'd expected him to send her away, if not taking her directly to jail.

She had not expected him to say in that same cool voice, 'Would you like to see him?'

It sucked the anger right out of her, leaving a cold fear sitting in the pit of her stomach. 'Him?' Her voice shook.

The hard lines of Galen's perfect face softened slightly. 'Our son. Leo.'

It felt as if a shard of glass had pierced her heart, an agony she tried to ignore yet it echoed through her all the same. And before she knew what she was doing, she'd shoved herself out of her chair and walked to the windows, turning away from him to hide the tears that filled her eyes.

Leo. Galen had named him.

You didn't. You didn't even think of a name.

Because she hadn't been able to think. Her head had felt foggy with postnatal hormones and shock. And solving the problem of how she was going to manage with a baby had seemed more important than finding a name for him.

There was silence behind her, then Galen said quietly, 'Leo is short for Leonidas. It is an old family name and it seems to suit him.'

She wanted to tell him she hated it, say how dare he name their child without her, but she didn't hate it. She liked it. A lot. It was only that she'd missed out on so much. He was nearly six months old now… Would he remember her?

He'll certainly remember the mother who gave him away to make her own life easier.

Solace squeezed her eyes shut, forcing away the tears and that terrible thought along with it. Because it wasn't true. It wasn't. She'd had to give him up. She'd had nothing to offer him, nothing at all, while Galen could give him a throne.

Abruptly, she was aware of a spicy, masculine scent, so close. He must be standing right behind her, though she hadn't heard him move.

She didn't want to turn around, not when there were still tears in her eyes, so she stayed where she was, resolutely turned away.

'Solace.' His deep voice whispered like rough velvet over her skin.

She could feel the warmth of his body and a part of her wanted to lean into it the way she had last night, surrender to him, let his strength hold her up because she felt so weak. But she couldn't. He'd taken her child and she was still furious about that and, besides, she had a battle ahead and she had to stay strong.

No weakness was permitted.

'Please don't come any closer.' She hoped her voice didn't sound as thick as she feared it did. 'And please…don't touch me.'

Another silence fell and then the scent was gone.

She swallowed, biting down on the urge to call him back, to tell him yes, please touch her, because she wanted to feel his hands on her again. Pleasure was always preferable to this pain. Yet that was another weakness she couldn't afford so she didn't.

The sound of papers shuffling came from behind her. 'I have ordered a car. We can be there in twenty minutes.'

Solace opened her eyes, blinking the remainder of her tears fiercely away and forcing the rest of her feelings to the side. Then, once she was feeling steadier, she turned.

Galen was back behind his desk as if he'd been there all along, his blue gaze giving nothing away.

'Where is there?' Solace asked, since that appeared to be the least problematic question.

'A residence of mine on the coast.'

She went cold. 'Not at the palace? But is it safe? He'd be much safer—'

'He has a retinue of twenty armed guards,' Galen interrupted mildly. 'He is more than safe. And the palace attracts far too much attention. I do not intend for him to live in a fishbowl.'

Solace fought down her fluttering panic. Of course, Galen would keep their son safe. Of course, he would. Their child was his heir, after all.

No, not 'their child'. *Leo*.

Another pang of grief hit her, but she ignored it. 'Okay,' she said with some reluctance, because she didn't want to agree with him, but, unfortunately, she did. 'That...seems like a good plan.'

There was something that looked like sympathy in Galen's eyes, and she wanted to turn away from it, but that felt too much like giving in, so she forced herself to bear it.

'He is safe,' Galen said with a gentleness that was almost painful. 'He is happy and well and growing like a weed.'

Tears threatened yet again, and again she forced them away. 'Good,' she said. 'I'm...glad.'

Galen's expression was impenetrable. 'Would you like to go now?'

Her voice seemed to have got stuck in her throat, but she managed a weak, 'Yes, please.'

He nodded and then strode from the room.

Solace was very tempted to sit back down in the chair since her legs felt wobbly, but she gritted her teeth and remained standing.

She was going to see him. She was going to see *him*. The son she hadn't even named. Because one minute she'd been trying to plan for the birth of a baby she'd had no idea she was even having, the next, she'd been in the ER with inexplicable stomach pain.

Except it hadn't been so inexplicable.

She'd had her little boy a few hours later and then had been sent home by the overworked nurses with a sheaf of pamphlets, and that had been it. He'd cried all night and she'd cried with him, because she hadn't had any idea what to do.

The people from Kalithera had arrived the next day.

Solace swallowed again and reached for her anger. It was the only thing that gave her strength, the only thing that got her through the mess her life had become, and that was no doubt about to get messier.

Then the door opened again, Galen standing in the doorway. 'Come. I have a car waiting.' His tone was neutral, his gaze running over her, assessing her.

She didn't like it. It made her uncomfortable. 'Don't look at me like that,' she said. 'I'm not a bomb about to go off, you know.'

If he was offended, he didn't show it. 'Evidently,' he murmured. 'Please, follow me.'

Snapping at him won't help.

Taking a deep breath, she let her grip on her anger loosen a bit then went to the door and followed Galen down the hallway to the entrance way.

Black-suited men waited discreetly outside as

she went down the steps to the nondescript car waiting at the bottom.

This time it was Galen who held the door open, waiting wordlessly for her to get in before getting in himself. He shut the door, enclosing them once again in the intimate space of the car.

Her breath caught, the delicious scent of his aftershave surrounding her, reminding her of everything that had happened the night before. Of his hands stroking her and his mouth tasting her. Of him inside her, creating the most intense pleasure between them. Of the weight of him on her and the way he'd held her down, and that terrible feeling of safety...

Prickles of heat washed over her, and she was very, very conscious of the long, powerful thigh almost but not quite touching hers and the seductive warmth of the man sitting next to her. Her mouth dried and she turned her head to look out of the window.

She didn't want to feel this, not now. She'd used their chemistry last night as a weapon, and, while she still could feel the desire coiling tight, it wasn't a weapon she wanted to use again.

Deep inside, threads of the ever-present shame and guilt wrapped around each other, but she forced them away. She'd done what she had to do, the way she always did. And anyway, it didn't matter now. Nothing mattered. Nothing mattered except she was going to see her son.

You don't deserve this. Not after what you did.

Solace closed her eyes, her nails digging into her palms where she held them in her lap, the pain driving the bitter thoughts away.

Then a sudden warmth covered her hands and she opened her eyes with a start, looking down to see one of Galen's large hands covering hers. He wore a heavy gold ring on his index finger, clearly very old and etched with vines and leaves growing around a crown.

His royal signet ring. A reminder of who he was.

She could feel the metal pressing lightly against her skin. It was warm. As warm as his hands were.

For a second, she didn't understand what he was doing. Was this an attempt at seduction and he meant to carry on what had happened between them the night before? But no. His hand didn't move to stroke or caress. He simply enclosed her icy fingers in his, the way he had that night at the gala after she'd dropped the tray.

Giving her comfort and reassurance.

She didn't want him to touch her like this. It frightened her. Mainly because something inside her desperately wanted his warmth, his touch, his strength. She wanted to be held, to be reassured. She wanted someone to tell her everything would be okay, because she was tired of every day being a battle.

But she knew what happened when she did that, when she trusted where she shouldn't. It always ended up with her suffering and she was tired of that too.

She wasn't sure why this man had the power to make her feel so weak, but she didn't like it and she didn't want it.

As if he could feel her tension, his hand squeezed hers gently. 'Don't be afraid. I'm not here to hurt you.'

'I'm not afraid.' She made as if to pull her hands from his, but he tightened his grip minutely.

'Relax,' he murmured as if she hadn't spoken. 'You're safe. Nothing will hurt you while you're with me. I will not allow it.'

There was a lump in her throat. His grip was very firm, and she doubted she could pull away without causing a fuss, though she could do that, obviously. If she really wanted to. Except… she didn't want to. It would take too much energy and, anyway, she could let herself have this, couldn't she? Just his hand holding hers?

It didn't mean anything, and it wasn't her giving her trust to him. It was a few moments of human contact, nothing major. And maybe it was even true, that nothing could harm her while he was here. After all, he'd told her she was safe the night before too, and she had been. Perhaps in this moment, she could believe him.

As if that thought was all her body needed, her muscles lost their tension and she felt herself sink into the softness of the seat cushions, let her hands beneath his soak up his warmth. But she kept her gaze firmly out of the window, because looking at him was a step too far.

Outside, the narrow streets of Therisos passed by, cobbled and twisted, ancient houses built from whitewashed stone all jumbled on top of one another. Stairs and alleyways snaked through the houses and streets—the city was famous for its historic architecture—while bougainvillea cascaded over walls and occasionally the green of a walled garden flashed by.

'I still think about that night,' Galen said unexpectedly, his deep voice quiet. 'That night at the ball with you.'

Shock gripped her. It had never occurred to her that he would still think about it, not once. She'd assumed she'd just been another in a long line of women he'd indulged himself with, despite how incredible it had been for her. 'Oh?' She tried to keep that shock from her voice.

'Yes,' he said. 'It was…remarkable. I wanted

to talk to you afterwards, but you ran away.' A pause. 'Did I frighten you?'

His tone was neutral and again, she found herself answering before she could think better of it. 'Not in the way you think. It was more... shock.'

'Ah,' he murmured.

'I hadn't... I don't usually...' She stopped then decided she might as well say it. 'You were my first.'

There was another long moment of silence.

Then Galen said, 'I was going to try to find you, but after the way you ran, it seemed obvious that you didn't want anything to do with me. There were lots of formalities I had to attend to that night as well, and so... I let you go.'

The lump in Solace's throat grew larger and it wouldn't go away no matter how many times she swallowed. What if she hadn't run? What if she'd stayed and he'd found her? She wouldn't have had to have their child alone...

You really think he'd have wanted anything to do with you? Especially when he found out who you were.

Well, he knew now, didn't he?

'It was probably for the best.' She tried to make her voice sound less hoarse and failed.

He didn't say anything to that, but after a moment his grip on her shifted and she felt him take one of her hands and turn it palm up. Then, with his thumb, he urged her fingers to uncurl and gently held them down.

Solace turned her head sharply in time to see him bend to press a kiss right in the centre of her palm.

A lightning strike of sensation went through her, and she almost gasped at the sensation of his lips, warm against her skin. Instinctively, she tried to pull away, but his grip was too strong, and when he lifted his head, there were deep blue sparks in his eyes.

A shudder went through her.

'Why did you do that?' she asked.

'It was a thank you.' His voice was slightly rough. 'For the gift.'

'What gift?'

'The gift of your body.' The sparks in his eyes became hotter. 'And of your virginity.'

Her face went hot. No one had thanked her for anything, still less a man she'd tried to blackmail a mere couple of hours or so earlier, and her instinct was to snap at him to cover her emotional reaction.

But he only smiled slightly, then let go of her hand. 'You'll forgive me. I have several calls to make.' And he reached into his pocket and took his phone out without another word.

Solace quickly turned back to the window,

her heart beating fast, though she wasn't sure why. She could still feel his kiss in the centre of her palm and before she could stop herself she'd curled her fingers around it as if to keep the warmth of it close to her skin.

Stupid. She didn't need to be thanked and she didn't need him to kiss her hand either. Yet she kept her fingers curled tight around that kiss as the car made its way along the coastline, past more modern housing developments and a few ancient villages.

Galen had several phone conversations, his deep voice almost hypnotic in its melodic rolling Kalitheran, and she found listening to him a great distraction from the strange ball of anxiety that had settled in her stomach.

Which only got worse as the car eventually slowed, pulling down a twisting, narrow lane that turned into an equally narrow, twisting driveway. Then it pulled up at a large, traditional, Kalitheran whitewashed villa perched on the side of a hill overlooking the sea. Terraced gardens surrounded it, with olives and cypresses, and she could see a couple of other small terraces that faced the sea beneath its terracotta roof.

After the car had come to a stop, Galen got out and held the door open for her. A light, fresh breeze caught the ends of her hair, filling the air with the scent of the sea and the distant sounds of waves crashing against rocks.

A peaceful, quiet place.

Better than your bedsit.

Yes, well. That wouldn't have been hard.

They moved towards the house, walking up a simple white stone path to the front door, which was then opened by a uniformed older woman who gave Galen a small bow. She murmured something in Kalitheran and Galen nodded.

The house was cool and quiet, all white walls and dark wooden floors, and it was peaceful, though the anxiety in Solace's stomach felt as if it were growing thorns and sticking into her, making it difficult to breathe.

Galen led her up a set of stairs and down a small hallway to a plain wooden door. Then he opened the door and went in.

Beyond it was a large room that faced the sea, and probably would have had magnificent views if the white linen curtains hadn't been drawn over the windows, turning the light diffuse and soft. A rustic but beautifully made wooden cot stood near a window, a mobile made of driftwood and shells turning slowly above it.

Solace froze in the doorway, the inexplicable anxiety wrapping around her throat and pulling tight.

Galen had paused beside the cot, looking

down at the small form inside it. He smiled and it was as if the sun had found its way into the room despite the curtains, the whole space lighting up. And all she could do was stare at him in astonishment, the anxiety momentarily forgotten in the face of that wonderful smile.

He loves your child too.

The thought resounded like a bell inside her and then was gone, because he leaned down, pulling away the blankets, before scooping up their baby with gentle hands, holding him as if he'd been holding babies all his life.

Then all thought left Solace entirely. Because there he was, cradled in Galen's arms, *her* child. Her baby boy. He'd grown so much.

Leo.

Pain throbbed behind her breastbone.

Galen glanced at her, his gaze luminous. 'Here he is. Come and say hello.'

Her legs felt weak and there was a part of her that didn't want to close the distance, that was afraid. As if once she touched him, he'd vanish. That he wouldn't be real, and this was all a dream. Or maybe that he'd look at her with accusing eyes, knowing what she'd done…

You don't deserve him anyway.

But it was that thought that drove her to move finally, coming over to where Galen stood. And then her arms were full of a warm burden and a little face was looking up into hers.

'He has your eyes,' Galen murmured.

A rush of the most powerful love swept over her in that moment, so intense she couldn't have spoken even if she'd wanted to. He was warm in her arms, and heavy, and he felt exactly as she'd remembered, and it was as if a piece of her soul had returned to her.

She stared down at him, not even noticing the tears running down her cheeks.

She didn't notice, either, when Galen slipped out of the room, leaving her alone with their child.

Galen closed the door of Leo's bedroom quietly and stood there, staring at the dark, polished wood, a fierce wave of emotion tightening in his chest.

An emotion he didn't want, yet had ignited the moment he'd seen the fear on Solace's pale face as she'd stood in the doorway. Then had tightened like barbed wire around his heart when she'd taken Leo in her arms, tears streaming down her face.

Guilt again. Guilt at what he'd taken from her. Guilt that he hadn't tried harder to find her once his son was safely at his side. And something else, something even more powerful that he couldn't name. Something to do with her holding Leo…the mother of his child holding his son…

They both belong to you.

Galen turned sharply from the door and strode down the hallway in the direction of the living area, where he could wait for her.

It was a ridiculous thought to have, like the one he'd had earlier, about marrying her. Yes, his son belonged to him, but Solace? He didn't know her so how could he possibly say? He wanted her physically, that was true, their chemistry was still there and still burning strong. He was going to need a mother for Leo and hopefully more children to secure the succession, so she would be a good choice of wife in that respect, considering she was actually Leo's mother. Also, since he wanted her, the getting of more children wouldn't be an issue.

But as he'd already thought, marrying her wasn't ideal either. Kostas would certainly have something to say about her suitability considering her origins, and how Galen wasn't following tradition. His past behaviour would no doubt be dredged back up, making things difficult, and there would be yet more talk about how unfit he was to rule, and how his contempt for Kalithera was clear in the woman he'd chosen to be his wife.

And then there was Solace's suitability for the role itself. She'd have no idea about what being the Queen of Kalithera meant. How her reputation had to be as spotless as his and she could not be seen to court media attention. There could be nothing in her background that would invite speculation, nothing in her behaviour either. She needed to be someone used to being in the public eye, too, and used to the pressure of being essentially public property.

Galen knew what was at stake. Could he afford to put his crown, not to mention his country in jeopardy for the sake of his guilt? Or even for the sake of Solace's feelings?

It *would* solve a great many of his problems, however.

He could put his PR department to work. Get them to create another story about her and where she came from. Perhaps explain that she hadn't died after all, and he'd reunited with her. It would be a sensational story and it would need to be rock solid to stand up to Kostas's scrutiny, but maybe he could swing it.

Are you really thinking of lying to your people yet again? So many lies...

Galen pushed his hands into the pockets of his trousers, staring out of the window at the rocky cliffs and the sea beyond, his jaw tight. Yes, another lie to fix another mistake. But he now had a debt towards her. He'd caused her a deep and lasting pain on top of a life that had been awful to start with, and, even apart from that, she was the mother of his child, and his child needed his mother.

His own had died not long after having him, and he'd always felt the lack. Especially when all he'd had was Alexandros, who'd actively hated him because he hadn't seen Galen as his son.

You might have been.

Tension crawled across Galen's shoulder blades. That was true. He *could* be Alexandros's son. He'd just never taken a DNA test to find out for certain, because if it was proved he wasn't the true King of Kalithera, he hadn't wanted any record of it anywhere. Better to go on assuming what everyone thought to be true, that he was Alexandros's son and heir, even if deep down he knew he wasn't. His father had hated him for a reason and that reason could only be that he wasn't his son.

Not that thinking about his father was a good use of his time now, not when he had more important problems to consider. Such as what he was going to do with Solace.

He stayed like that, staring out towards the sea, turning plans over in his head, until he heard someone say his name.

Turning, he saw Solace standing in the doorway. She had her hands clasped together and the vibrating anxiety he'd sensed in her in the car, that he'd put his hand over hers to try to calm, had gone. In its place was a determination even more steely than she'd radiated in his office earlier.

Her grey eyes met his, sharp as a shard of glass. 'I am not leaving him. Never, *ever* again.'

Again, he was conscious of the respect she'd earned from him earlier, with her stubborn insistence on fighting for their child, only deepening. It complicated things that she was so set on being with Leo, but all he could think of was how fierce she looked. A small white tiger baring her teeth in defence of her cub. And how he liked that. How it made the desire inside him, that was still there no matter how he tried to ignore it, begin to coil and tighten once more.

He'd thought taking her to see Leo had been the right thing to do, a way to at least start to put right the wrongs that had been done to her, all the while suspecting that seeing her child would only entrench her determination. Sure enough, it had. But he wasn't as unhappy about that as he'd expected. In fact, it had even cleared a few things up.

Yes, why not marry her? He could handle his uncle, and his PR department would do the rest, then his son would have his mother back while he could have a woman in his bed that he had magnificent chemistry with and whom he could have whenever he wanted. This was the one solution that would fix all the mistakes he'd made and put right the wrong he'd done to her.

You think lying to your people to cover up all your errors is any better? It'll only make every-thing worse. And what will happen if anyone finds out what you've done?

Nothing would happen. Because no one would find out. He'd make sure of it.

And yes, it would mean yet another lie, but there were no good choices here. This solution would ensure Kalithera stayed protected even if something happened to him while his uncle was still alive.

'Good,' he said crisply. 'I wouldn't want the mother of my child to act in any other way.'

Clearly expecting a fight, she blinked in surprise.

Which pleased him. He did like surprising a woman. In fact, now he'd made the decision to marry her, he was very tempted to prowl closer, circle her, see what she'd do. Whether she'd give him a chase or face him, those sharp claws of hers bared. Either would suit him. Either would make him hard.

However, it was not the time or the place, not

with his son upstairs, so he remained where he was, his hands in his pockets. 'And if you're to marry me, you'll have to remain in Kalithera anyway.'

Her eyes went wide and this time it wasn't surprise that rippled over her features, but shock. 'Marry you? What?'

'I think you heard me.' He put authority in his voice, the weight of the crown behind the words. 'I've been considering finding a wife for some time now, mainly because our son needs a mother, but also to secure the succession. However there has been a distinct lack of suitable candidates. At least, there was until last night.' He took a couple of steps towards her, unable to help himself. 'I suspect that you'll do nicely. After all, what better woman to be Leo's mother than his mother herself?'

Solace had gone very pale, her hands in a white-knuckled grip in front of her. 'You can't mean that.'

Galen lifted a brow. 'Why can't I mean that?'

'I'm a nobody, I told you. I don't know who my parents were. I was raised in the foster system, and I dropped out of high school. I... I... have been arrested for shoplifting a couple of times...' She stopped, breathing hard.

'You seem to think that I don't know every single thing about you, Solace Ashworth,' Galen said calmly. 'But I do. None of this is a surprise to me and none of it matters. The press will be told some story about your origins and no doubt we can come up with some reason why the mother of my child is apparently alive and well. They'll be so busy with our apparent emotional reuniting to be bothered about whether it's true or not.'

She took a couple of steps forward, silver eyes glittering. 'No, you can't mean that. I'm not a... I'm not a *queen*.'

He strolled to meet her in the middle of the room, getting closer once again to the fierce passion that burned in her face and the delicate heat of her body. He shouldn't and he knew it, but he couldn't stop himself. She was irresistible.

'I disagree,' he said. 'You have fought me at every turn since this morning and been nothing but strong and courageous and fierce. Isn't that what a queen is?'

'A queen isn't a nobody,' she insisted. 'A queen isn't a foster kid with no money and no education and no prospects.'

'A queen is whoever I say she is and if I say she's you then she's you.'

'But I don't even know you!'

He lifted a shoulder. 'So? We'll have time to get to know each other. Besides, the most important thing is compatibility in bed, and we have that in spades.'

Her mouth opened then shut and suddenly all he wanted to do was to take her pretty face between his hands and cover that mouth with his own, taste her again. He'd been hoping this morning for more time in bed, at least until her ill-advised blackmail attempt, and now he was reminded again of how good she'd felt in his arms and how sweet her surrender had been.

He wanted more. He wanted to pull the ties of that pretty sundress she wore, let it fall from her body then take her down on the rugs right here in the living room. Perhaps he'd tie her wrists with it. She'd liked being restrained by him. She'd liked it very much.

From the looks of the two spots of high colour that glowed in her cheeks, she wouldn't have protested if he had. Plus, he could tell by how fixedly she was staring at him that she wanted to look at his mouth, the way she did when she was aroused.

But no. He wouldn't touch her yet. She needed to sit with the idea, and she definitely needed more time with their son. That would help clarify things for her.

'I could be his nanny,' she burst out. 'I could be his nurse or—'

'He has a nanny. Not to mention a fleet of

nurses. The one thing he does not have is a mother.'

She shook her head. 'No. No, it's impossible.'

It would be interesting to press her about why exactly it was so impossible, but he was conscious that he'd spent more time than he'd intended with her this morning and his schedule for today was already crowded. He needed to return to the palace and quickly.

So, perhaps a week, maybe two for her to get comfortable here. For her to consider his proposal. Not that it was really a proposal, more of a command. Then he would bring her to the palace so they could discuss it further.

Maybe he'd even fulfil his promise of last night to her, of a seduction. In fact, now he thought of it, he couldn't think of anything he'd rather do. He hadn't had the opportunity to seduce a woman in too many years, and, really, it was just the kind of challenge he liked.

'Well,' he said gently, 'since I decide what is impossible and what is not, we will have to agree to differ on that.' He paused, allowing some steel to show in his expression. 'It is also not a request.'

He thought she might take a step back at that, but she didn't. She only stood there, staring at him as if she'd never seen him before in her life. And he could see it then, the legacy of her hard, difficult life. It was there in the anger that glittered brightly in her eyes, and in the stubborn line of her jaw. The bravery of a woman who would not lie down or give up, a woman who'd fought and struggled for everything she had.

Yes, she would make an excellent queen.

'You're crazy,' Solace said. 'I'm not marrying you.'

Galen smiled. 'We'll see.' He stepped back, giving them both some space, because if he remained this close to her any longer, he'd probably do something he'd regret. 'I'll arrange for you to remain here with Leo and you can spend as much time with him as you wish. Though, I must insist on you not speaking with the staff. Your identity must remain secret until this is sorted out. They'll be informed that you're a family member and will need access to him at all times.'

Her jaw had that stubborn line to it again. 'Send them all away. I'll care for him myself.'

It was on the tip of his tongue to refuse since his staff were excellent. But then he paused. Perhaps having her looking after Leo was best. It would mean he wouldn't need to explain why one of Leo's family members had suddenly appeared and also wouldn't have to be concerned about any potential gossip.

'Very well,' he allowed. 'I'll get Maria, his

nanny, to leave you all the information about him, as well as contact details for anything you might need yourself.' He turned towards the door. 'I'll send for you when the time comes.'

'Send for me for what? What time?'

He paused at the doorway and smiled. 'The time for you to agree to my proposal.' Then he walked through it before she could speak.

CHAPTER SIX

SOLACE WRAPPED LEO up in his blanket and cradled him in her arms, rocking him gently. She'd just given him his evening feed, a bath and put him in a fresh onesie, and was in the process of putting him to bed.

It was evening, the sunset painting the sky with brilliant oranges and reds and golds, and she stood by the window in his room, watching it as she hummed a soft lullaby.

From the moment she'd first taken him in her arms and his big grey eyes had looked up into hers—Galen had been right, Leo *did* have her eyes—the rest of the world had fallen away. All her fury, all her pain, everything she'd been through, none of it had mattered. The only thing that had was the baby she held. *Her* baby.

Finally, she had him. Finally, he was here where he belonged, safe in her arms. And it had been worth it. In that moment, everything—*everything*—she'd gone through had been worth it.

Galen had left to give her privacy and she'd been desperately grateful to him for that, because all she'd been able to do was hold her son and weep. Weep with grief and guilt for all the moments she'd lost, yet also with dizzying joy that she'd be with him for all the moments still to come. And the relief, the sheer, aching relief that he was safe and well and she was with him again.

Then had followed the happiest week of her life, with nothing to worry about and nothing to do except be with Leo.

She'd spent days lying with him on a blanket in amongst the olive trees, or with him in her arms on the couch in the living room, reading him a book. Or singing. Or showing him white pebbles or flowers or long stalks of green grass in the garden.

She didn't have to worry about money or a job, or how she was going to get nappies or food, or whether the bills had been paid and her electricity was going to get cut off. Everything was provided for her, whatever she asked for was delivered.

Her things from the hostel she'd been staying in had appeared in one of the bedrooms the day after she'd arrived, and, sure enough, Maria, Leo's nanny, had left her a little book full of notes about Leo and his likes and dislikes.

What his early months had been like and what kind of baby he was. There were even photos.

Solace had cried over that little book, again for everything she'd missed out on, yet also for what had been given back to her, and it had taken a few days for that to stop hurting. A couple of times she'd demanded frivolous things just to see if Galen really was as good as his word and anything she wanted would be given to her, and indeed they had been.

She'd worried off and on about his ridiculous proposal of marriage and what would happen in the future, and then, because it felt too hard to think about, she'd pushed all of that to the back of her mind, because right now Leo was more important and she wanted to spend her time thinking about him, not the future.

He was such a good baby, calm and rarely fussy, with lots of smiles. The first time he'd smiled at her, she'd thought her heart would burst with joy.

He smiled up at her now as she rocked him, staring up at her as if entranced.

She smiled back, love for him making her chest ache, and then she lifted him for a snuggle. He gave the most delightful gurgling laugh that made tears start in her eyes.

Really, it was a good thing she'd been completely alone with him for the past week given the amount of time she'd spent weeping. She cried more than he did.

Don't get too complacent. This could all come crashing down at any minute.

Oh, she knew that. But a week to allow herself some happiness, to exist in the moment with her child, didn't seem like too big an ask.

Still humming her lullaby, Solace gently laid Leo down in his cot and adjusted his blankets. He generally went down without a fuss, and he must have been extra sleepy today because his eyes closed almost as soon as she'd laid a kiss on his forehead.

She tiptoed out of the room, pulling the door to, and then went down the hallway. She was on the point of coming down the stairs when she heard car tyres crunch on the gravel driveway outside.

Everything inside her tensed.

She'd been alone for the entire week, apart from a security detail so discreet she barely saw them. No one had bothered her. She'd half expected Galen to visit, but he hadn't. She hadn't heard from him for days.

Then only the day before one of Galen's aides had arrived with an invitation for her to come to the palace the next day. It was her summons, just as he'd said.

A car would be sent, along with Maria to

look after Leo. It was merely a casual dinner to discuss his earlier proposal, nothing too formal. However, with the summons he'd also sent three dresses that had been chosen with her in mind, since he knew she wouldn't have anything suitable. Dresses that could in no way could be termed 'casual'.

She'd been angry at his high-handedness, all the while sitting on the bed in the bedroom hardly daring to touch the expensive fabric of the dresses laid on the bed. She'd never had such pretty things to choose from before. She'd never had pretty things at all. Everything she had was the cheapest she could buy and there was never anything left over for luxuries.

But these dresses…one in ice-blue silk, another in white satin, a third in tailored black velvet. They were all glamorous and sophisticated, sexy but subtle, nothing like her dress of silver mesh, which was not subtle in the least.

Part of her didn't want to wear the dresses because he'd chosen them and he obviously meant her to wear one, and she hated the thought of accepting his charity. Then again, she loved them, and she didn't know when she'd get another chance to wear something like them again, so why not? It wasn't charity. It was dressing for the occasion. Also, she rather liked the idea of turning him down while wearing something beautiful, because of course she was going to turn him down.

His whole idea was ludicrous. Marry a man she barely knew and not just any man, but a king. And she would become his queen. It was like something out of a fairy tale or a dream, not something that would ever—*ever*—in a million years happen to someone like her. Naturally, she couldn't trust the idea, not one bit.

Even if a part of her wanted it so badly she ached.

To have a home and a family, and not just any home and family, but one in a palace, with a king for a husband. She wouldn't need to worry about rent or having enough money for food. She'd have her baby with her and a whole garrison of palace guards to keep everyone safe...

And she'd have him. Galen standing between her and the world, standing between her and everything that could hurt her. Galen holding her at night, giving her the most incredible pleasure. He'd made her feel so good...

Her heart throbbed, a tugging ache.

It's too good to be true. You can't trust it.

She knew that. If Katherine, the foster mother she'd wanted to stay with, could change her mind about her for no apparent reason, then why couldn't Galen? He was only offering to marry her because of Leo anyway. He'd never have chosen her if not for that.

No, it was better not to accept anything so out of the realms of possibility as a marriage proposal from him. It was a dream. And the problem with dreams was that you always woke up. Always.

Still, all of that didn't mean she had to forgo a nice dress, and, since they were here anyway, she might as well wear one.

She decided on the ice-blue silk, since it had a lace bodice that left her shoulders bare and a frothy skirt with a hem that fell to her calves at the back while it ended at her knees at the front. There were strappy, high-heeled sandals in ice blue to match, and, with her hair falling loose around her shoulders, she felt like a fairy princess.

It was a shameless indulgence, but why not? Hadn't she earned it?

She waited for the car and when it arrived, she greeted Maria and spent a moment with her discussing Leo's needs for the evening. Maria had looked after Leo since he'd been brought to Kalithera and she loved him too, which Solace had found immensely comforting.

Reassured by Maria's competent presence at Leo's side, Solace then strode from the house and got into the car.

Nerves fluttered in her gut as the car wound up the driveway to the coastal road, but she tried to ignore them. Except the flutter grew more intense the closer to Therisos they got, until it felt as if there were a million butterflies all crowding for space inside her.

She didn't know why, when there was nothing to be nervous about. Except it wasn't only nervousness. She was also conscious of something that felt like excitement fluttering there too, and anticipation. As if she were looking forward to seeing him again, which surely couldn't be right when she hardly knew him.

Except she'd had dreams this past week, of blue eyes and strong hands, and a delicious hot, heavy weight pressing her down. And she'd wake up restless and sweaty, the sheet sticking to her, an ache throbbing gently between her thighs.

You still want him.

Maybe, but that wasn't the same as being excited to see him. Wanting him was physical, that was all, and it certainly didn't mean she was going to agree to marry him.

The royal palace in Therisos was set on a hill above the town, looking out towards the ancient city walls that protected the city from the sea. It was built of white stone and at night was lit up, so it looked as if its towers and terraces floated above the city like a castle out of dreams.

Solace put a hand over the butterflies in her stomach, trying to settle them as the car got clearance from the guards at the palace gates and was driven through, winding up the avenue to the palace itself.

It was imposing, white towers soaring high, topped with the Kalitheran flag moving slowly in the night breeze from the sea.

As she stepped out of the car, a liveried palace servant greeted her and led her up the grand white stairs and into the palace.

Her heartbeat had accelerated, and her mouth was dry, the butterflies in her stomach now numbering in their thousands. But she ignored the feelings. Silly to feel this way about a man she'd only met a couple of times. A man she'd had the most intense night of pleasure with, it was true. Yet he was also the man who'd taken her son from her and that still hurt. Marriage to him was an impossibility and she had no problems telling him that.

She was led through grand halls of plain, whitewashed stone, the walls dotted here and there with paintings of what she assumed were past royals. Galen's lineage, she suspected. An ancient line, ancient blood. Royalty going back centuries.

Solace couldn't imagine her portrait hanging anywhere in these halls. The thought was
ludicrous. A hundred pictures of ancient kings
and queens, and one of a poor single mother
from London.

The servant led her up a wide staircase and
down a hall to some huge doors that led out
onto a wide terrace, bounded in white stone
that looked out towards the sea. Then Solace
stopped in the doorway, shocked.

A delicate pergola covered the terrace and
fairy lights had been wound all through it, creating a warm, diffuse light. A table stood off to
one side, set with a white tablecloth, silver cutlery and crystal glasses. Candles stood around
the terrace, on the wall edging it and at various
points on the white stone floor, flames flickering and dancing, illuminating the tall figure of
a man standing at the edge of the terrace, his
back to her.

Galen.

Solace wasn't aware of the servant discreetly
withdrawing behind her, or of anything else.
Every sense she had seemed to be concentrated
on the man on the terrace. On his broad back
and wide, muscled shoulders. His narrow waist
and powerful legs.

He wore black tonight, the way he had a week

ago in the club. Simple clothes that only high-lighted his mouth-watering physique.

There was a rushing sound in her head, a trembling that started up deep inside her, that wouldn't go away no matter how hard she tried to force it. The same visceral reaction she always had to the sight of this man, her body wanting his so badly she could hardly stand it.

Slowly, he turned around and the trembling got worse the moment his blue eyes met hers.

He was beautiful. He was devastating. He was a king and far too much for the likes of her, and if she wasn't careful, he would overwhelm her as he had the last couple of times.

She'd thought that after a week of not being around him her reaction to him wouldn't be so intense, but she was wrong. If anything, a week's absence had made her want him more.

The light of a dozen candles flickered over his face, illuminating the perfection of his cheek-bones, the straight line of his nose, and the curve of his beautiful mouth.

He smiled and abruptly it washed over her like a wave where she'd seen that smile before: his son had it too.

He will break your heart. They both will.

The thought was fleeting, because then the smile gradually faded and heat leapt instead in his midnight-blue eyes. And she could feel the air between them start to crackle, their chemistry on the verge of igniting like dry tinder.

Galen started towards her, moving like a predatory jungle cat, and she froze, utterly unable to move. Her heartbeat was careening out of control and dimly a part of her was astonished at how quickly she'd gone from being steely and determined, to melting like tar seal under a hot sun. That part of her screamed at her to resist him, to be on her guard, and hadn't she learned that she couldn't trust him?

But before she could even make that choice, he came to an abrupt stop, his hands clenching, his whole body taut. A muscle jumped in the side of his hard jaw. He looked like a man who had himself on a leash so tight it was choking him.

'Solace.' His deep voice was as tight as the rest of him, his eyes blazing a bright searing blue. 'Welcome to the palace.'

She trembled, aching to close the distance between them and feel the touch of his hands, his mouth. Be once again in his arms, surrounded by that wonderful sense of warmth and safety, experiencing that pleasure.

But she couldn't trust him, she couldn't. So, she stayed where she was.

'What—?' She had to clear her throat and

start again. 'What's all this? The candles, the lights…'

'It's for you.' He stood rigid, his gaze intense on hers. 'You are here for dinner, remember?'

'You said a casual dinner.'

'It is casual. But I wanted it to be special as well.'

She looked at him blankly. 'Special? Why?'

'It's only been a week, Solace.' That muscle in the side of his jaw jumped again. 'You must remember that I want you to marry me.'

Solace blinked, trying to get her brain working. Marriage, that was right, and she'd been going to refuse. She'd been determined, even. Yet…all these candles, all these lights… It was so pretty. A white tablecloth and fine crystal. Silver cutlery.

He'd wanted it to be special, he'd said.

It was stupid to feel so emotional over some candles and fairy lights, and a nicely set table. It was just… He'd made an effort for her, and no one had ever done that before. No one since Katherine and the princess bed Katherine had been going to buy for her. To go in her new room, Katherine had said. 'A princess bed for my little princess'.

Solace had never wanted anything so badly in all her life. A princess bed just for her. She'd been so thrilled. Then Katherine had changed her mind and hadn't wanted Solace after all. She'd been given no reason, only that Katherine had changed her mind about a formal adoption. So back she had gone to another family, and there had been no princess bed for her.

But now, here, it wasn't only a bed she was being offered, but a man she wanted, a man who gave her pleasure, and a palace, a place of safety. A crown, even. And Leo.

How could she refuse? And it would give Leo what she'd never had: a family.

He took your child. How can you ever forget that?

Maybe she couldn't. Maybe it wasn't possible to forget. And maybe this *was* too good to be true and Galen wasn't to be trusted and she shouldn't agree to it. Or maybe she could put her anger aside and have this anyway, and if it all fell apart in the end, at least she'd have the memory of it. Wasn't that better than the memory of a bed she'd never even got to sleep in?

'Yes,' she said. 'Yes, I remember.'

His blue gaze roamed over her as if he couldn't help himself. 'Well? What is your answer?'

There was only one answer she could give, and she knew it. But it wouldn't hurt him to make him wait for it.

'I don't know yet.' Her chin lifted and she gave him a challenging look. 'Convince me.'

Something in Galen's eyes flared, as if he'd been waiting for her to say that all along, and he strode forward, crossing that aching distance between them and stopping in front of her. 'And how do you wish to be convinced?' The rough edge in his voice left no doubt in her mind about what kind of convincing he wanted.

Luckily it was exactly the sort she wanted too.

She met his gaze squarely, letting him see the intensity that blazed inside her. 'I think you know.'

He didn't wait. He lifted his hands and took her face between them and she didn't pull away. And when he tipped her head back and covered her mouth with his, her own hands lifted helplessly, her fingers threading in his hair.

And everything fell away.

There was nothing in the world but this kiss, full of heat and desire and longing.

Nothing in the world but the warmth of his body and the delicious spice of his scent.

He is everything you dreamed about in the lonely darkness. Everything you've ever wanted.

Perhaps that was even true. He was certainly everything she wanted right now.

His mouth on hers was hungry, exploring her, tasting her as if she'd been lost to him for years and now he'd found her again, he was hell-bent on familiarising himself with every single part of her.

She couldn't resist him, not even if she tried. Though she wasn't going to try. They were like magnets, helplessly drawn to each other, unwilling to be torn apart.

His fingers pushed into her hair, tipping her head back further, the kiss deepening, turning hotter and more feverish. Stripping everything away, all her anger, all her fight. Yet for some reason, tonight her passion didn't make her feel exposed or vulnerable. No, tonight there was a strength in it. Because, for all his power, he was as much a slave to this white-hot chemistry as she was. Just as helpless. In fact, the whole reason she was even here right now was because of his inability to resist her.

You've always had that power over him.

She liked that idea very much.

Galen tore his hands from her hair and lifted her up in his arms, and then she was being carried over to a bench covered with thick cushions. He put her down on the edge, then pushed her knees apart so he could kneel between them. And he kissed her, his hands stroking over her neck and her shoulders, tracing the lines of her collarbones and then pulling at the delicate ice-blue lace of her dress, easing it away and down.

'Galen,' she whispered against his mouth as he tugged the fabric down to her waist, his fingers stroking the curves of her bare breasts, making her shiver.

His lips moved from hers, following the path of his hands, down her neck to the hollow of her throat, tasting her. 'Yes, silver girl?' he murmured. 'What do you want? Tell me.'

But she couldn't think of why she'd said his name. Maybe it had only been for the pleasure of it. And as for what she wanted... 'Don't stop,' she whispered. 'Please.'

He gave a soft laugh. 'Oh, believe me, I have no intention of stopping.' As if to prove it, his hands settled lightly at the small of her back, making her spine arch, and then his mouth was on her breast, sucking and teasing her nipple, biting gently and making her moan.

Then he pushed her against the back of the seat, spreading her thighs wider, her dress up around her hips. He pulled her to the edge, tearing off her lacy underwear, and then his fingers were pressing apart the delicate folds of her sex. He bent, his breath against her sensitive flesh, and then his tongue exploring her.

Solace cried out, her fingers buried in his hair as the bonfire of pleasure built inside her, making her shake. His hands held her thighs firmly apart and down, pinning her to the cushions, holding her there so he could taste her lightly at first then deeper, with firm strokes of his tongue.

The pleasure built so quickly she was on the brink of ecstasy before she even knew what was happening, her whole body shaking. He kept her there for what seemed like eons, drawing out the moment endlessly, until she was writhing on the cushions, desperate for him to finish it, saying his name over and over like a prayer.

Then his strong, capable hands tightened further, and his tongue pressed hard and firm on the place where she needed it most and she was flying up into the night sky, only to burst like a firework in a bright explosion of glory.

Galen felt Solace's body shake, his name a desperate cry that echoed in the night air and he allowed himself the deep, primal satisfaction that came with it in response.

This was not how he'd planned for this night to go. He hadn't thought that everything would completely vanish from his head the moment he turned around and saw her standing in the doorway.

Yet it had.

Her hair had been loose over her shoulders, and she was wearing one of the dresses he'd picked out for her personally, the blue one, which happened to be his favourite. And it looked as fantastic on her as he'd thought it would, the lace showcasing beautifully her pale shoulders and neck, while the uneven hemline made the most of her pretty legs.

She'd looked ethereal and lovely, and the kick of desire had taken him utterly by surprise. It shouldn't have. He should have known that need would be lying in wait, ready for the moment when their eyes would meet and it would flare into life, burning through every good intention he had.

He'd wanted to seduce her, first with food and conversation, and then, when he'd got her agreement to the marriage, because of course she'd agree, he'd seduce her with his body. Show her exactly how good being married to him would be.

A foolproof plan, he'd thought.

Until he'd taken one look at her and that plan had burned to the ground.

He'd tried to stop himself. God knew, his whole life had been nothing but try and try and try. But when it came to her, no matter how many warnings or assurances he gave himself, that this time he'd stay in control, that this time he'd resist, he always forgot every single one the moment he laid eyes on her.

She'd given him that direct look, and it had

been full of heat. Then challenged him to convince her, and he'd been lost.

He hadn't understood how hungry he'd been for her until her fingers had pushed into his hair and she'd kissed him back. And he was hungry still, even now, kneeling between her silky thighs with the delicious, sweet flavour of her on his tongue. He needed more than this taste. He needed to be inside her and right now.

She'd sagged back against the bench, her face flushed, her mouth slightly open, and the sight of her only honed his hunger to a sharper edge.

'Solace.' Her name came out as a growl, but he didn't try to stop it as he rose to his feet. It was meant to be a question, yet he couldn't quite get out the rest. There was nothing but demand left in him.

Her silver eyes were lit up by the candles and the fairy lights above, and he felt something tighten behind his breastbone that had nothing to do with the other tightness he felt down below his belt.

She was so very lovely, a woman made of starlight and silver, and delicate-seeming. Yet there was heat inside her. Heat and a strength that he found just as sexy as the rounded shape of her breasts or the slick softness between her thighs.

And also an aching vulnerability that made

him want to gather her up and hold her in his arms, protect her from everything that might harm her. He wasn't sure why he was feeling such things about a woman he didn't know, but he felt them. It was as if his body already knew her, and his mind was taking its time to catch up.

Her gaze focused on him and then unexpectedly she lifted her arms, and the painful tension inside him relaxed. Then he was pressing her down on the cushioned bench, settling between her warm thighs, and he was surrounded in the delicious, lightly musky scent of aroused woman.

He pushed a hand down between them, stroking her, making her gasp and sigh once again, her hips undulating against his. Her hands were pressed to his chest, her fingers curled into the fabric of his shirt, and she lifted her head, finding his mouth. Such a sweet kiss. She was so passionate, all that ferocity and anger turned into heat. It was glorious and he wanted it.

His childhood had been so cold, Alexandros demanding and exacting. He'd never touched Galen, not once. Not a hug or even a handshake. There was no closeness, no warmth, only a thinly veiled loathing that sometimes Galen felt like a poison deep in his heart.

But his life would never be cold if she was in it. There would be arguments and fights aplenty, yet then there would also be passionate reconciliations…

She would fight for you if she were yours. She fights hard for the things she loves.

And she did. She'd fought for Leo, coming all the way to Kalithera with her blackmail plan. He hadn't met a woman like her. Even the few he'd managed discreet liaisons with had all tried to turn themselves into what he wanted them to be, but not her. Never her. She wasn't afraid of him and even when she'd seduced him the week before, she'd been nothing but herself.

Galen undid his trousers, suddenly desperate, then reached for her hand, pushing it down between them. 'Put me inside you, silver girl,' he ordered. 'I want you to do it.'

There were sparks in her eyes, the pretty flush in her cheeks creeping down her throat. 'I don't take orders.'

'You'll take mine,' he murmured. 'And you'll like it.' Then he flexed his hips, pressing into her hand.

She gave a little moan. 'Galen…'

'You know what to do.' He bent and bit the side of her neck gently. 'So do it and put us both out of our misery.'

Her fingers tightened around him, the slight pressure driving him half out of his mind, then she was guiding him to her and easing him inside, her slick, hot flesh parting for him so sweetly.

She shuddered beneath him as he pushed in deeper, her gaze on his, glittering like stars. And he was caught by how intense this moment was, how it always was with her and only with her. She'd looked at him like this that night at the gala, just like this. With wonder and pleasure and a certain kind of awe that made the man in him want to growl with satisfaction. She'd looked at him like this that night in his limo too.

Perhaps she would always look at him this way and perhaps the expression on his face would always be the same.

There was a connection between them on some deep level he couldn't articulate, that went beyond merely physical. Maybe even beyond the blood tie they had in Leo. He had never believed in such things, but he believed when it involved her.

'Well?' he demanded roughly. 'Are you convinced yet? Marry me and we'll be together every night, just like this.'

'Galen…' She shifted, arching up, trying to get him to move. 'Please…'

'Only if you say yes.' He kept still, though it took everything he had, holding her brilliant gaze with his. She'd used their chemistry to get what she wanted and now it was his turn. He would have this. He would have her in his bed and his people would have a queen, and, most importantly, his son would have his mother. 'I will have you, silver girl. You are mine.'

She gave a breathless sigh and then, as she had in the limo the day he'd taken her to see Leo, when he'd put his hand over hers and had felt all the fight slowly melt out of her, she melted beneath him now. Her hands pulled him down, her legs tightening around his waist. 'Yes,' she murmured against his mouth. 'Yes, I'll marry you.'

Satisfaction filled him and he bent to kiss her hard, allowing himself to move at last. He drove himself into her, feeling her grip him, so hot and so tight, keeping him exactly where he wanted to be.

He pulled her hands from his shirt and held them down beside her head, because he liked restraining her, liked her wriggling and writhing pinned beneath him. And he knew she liked that too, because her eyes were dark with desire and her thighs gripped him the way her sex gripped him, as if she didn't want to let him go.

He drove harder, faster, taking them both higher, until he was drowning in pleasure, drowning in the feel of her body and the sounds of her gasps in his ears, in the heat that was being generated between them.

The orgasm came like a tidal wave, roaring through him, sweeping away all thought and all awareness, crushing him utterly beneath the relentless onslaught of pleasure.

It took him long moments to gather himself together again and shift to give her space to breathe. But he kept his fingers around her wrists, though he loosened his hold. He wanted her to remember what she'd promised him, because, even after that, he did.

'You had some hesitations about marrying me,' he said after some time had passed. 'I want to know why.'

Her eyes were closed, blonde lashes lying still on her cheeks. 'Does it matter?'

'Yes, of course it matters. Ours isn't a marriage of convenience, Solace. It will be a true marriage and, since we aren't familiar with each other, I think we should start getting acquainted.'

Her lashes lifted, her eyes still darkened with the aftermath of pleasure, and she studied him a moment. Then she said, 'Yes, I have hesitations, though it isn't any mystery as to why. You know all about my background, Galen. Why do you think I'd have doubts about marrying a king?'

'I think many people in your position would have no doubts whatsoever. Not when they can have all the power, money, social standing they desire.'

She shook her head. 'Money is useful, I won't deny that, and power…well, I've never had any so I can see the attraction. And as for social standing, I don't care about that at all.'

Galen stared down at her, aware of his own growing curiosity. Her file had given him, as she'd said, knowledge of her background, but nothing else. He wanted to know more. He wanted to know where she'd found her backbone of steel and the flames of her anger, and the drive he could sense in her.

She hadn't let her background crush her and he wanted to know why not.

'Then why?' He searched her face. 'Is it because you and I don't know each other?'

'No.' She let out a slow breath. 'I've told you already. I told you last week. I'm a nobody, Galen. I don't know who my parents were, yet you have a whole line of portraits of your ancestors that go back hundreds of years.'

If only she knew. Luckily, she didn't. Yet he didn't think that her unknown parentage was the issue here, or not the main issue. There was something else going on.

He studied the shifting emotional currents in her gaze. 'What are you afraid of?'

Instantly she scowled. 'I am not afraid, I'm just not the type—'

'Don't lie to me,' he interrupted. 'I can see the fear in your eyes.'

She looked away, her lashes sweeping down, her body tensing beneath him. It was clear she did not want to talk about this and maybe, at a different time, he wouldn't have pursued it.

But she was going to be his queen, which meant he needed to know. He needed to know everything about her, her dreams and her hopes, and, yes, her fears too.

'If you think I'm going to let this go, you're mistaken,' he said.

'I don't have to tell you if I don't want to.'

He released one of her wrists and took her chin in his hand, turning her to face him and holding her there. 'Yes,' he insisted. 'You do.'

'I don't—'

'Remember what I told you in the nightclub? About being able to trust me?'

Her gaze sharpened like a spear. 'You took my baby, Galen. You took him away from me. And that hurt. It *hurt*. How can I ever trust you after that?'

That spear slid beneath his skin, a sharp pain stabbing deep.

There had been many misunderstandings in the aftermath of Leo's birth, but, ultimately, he was the one who'd made the mistakes, starting with the fact that he hadn't worn a condom. Then he'd taken Leo away, thinking the worst of her, that she'd given him up in favour of money. Then he'd lost track of her so that she'd had to spend six months desperately trying to get her son back, all the while suffering postnatal depression.

She had lost everything because of him.

You took a crown that wasn't yours to take and then you took a child...

The spear slid deeper, into his heart.

She was right not to trust him. In her place, he wouldn't trust him either.

'I know,' he said. 'I know. And you have every right not to trust me. But...' He paused and held her gaze, letting the intensity of his regret blaze in his. 'I'm sorry for what I did, Solace. You will never know how sorry. I shouldn't have taken him from you, and I shouldn't have assumed the worst of you. I shouldn't have let you fall through the cracks and be forgotten. And I can promise you now, my word as a king, that I will *never* take Leo from you or you from him, not ever again.'

Her silver gaze cut him into shreds and he let her. He'd never let anyone study him so completely before and it wasn't comfortable, but he let her. He had the sense that if he didn't, she might not ever give him her trust and, if this was going to work between them, he needed it. And that a clear demonstration was required.

'People say things,' she said. 'People say things all the time about how they can be trusted, and they always lie.'

The tight feeling in his chest tightened even more. 'What people?'

'Foster parents. Social workers. Government officials. I...' She broke off as if afraid of saying too much.

'You what?' He could feel the tension in her jaw, as if she was trying to pull away from his fingers, so he tightened his grip. He didn't want her to pull away. That would only delay this conversation and he didn't want to delay it. He was hungry for knowledge, everything about her, everything her background report hadn't said.

The look in her eyes now was pure defiance, her defensive anger leaping. 'I don't know you, yet you want to marry me, and I don't understand it. I don't trust it. No one has ever wanted me before so what makes you any different?'

Galen was conscious of a small, bright ache behind his ribs. As if part of him knew exactly what that felt like. Because even though he hadn't known the reason until later, he'd never forgotten the way Alexandros used to look at him. There had been no love there, only fury. Galen had never been a son to Alexandros, only a cuckoo in the nest.

Sometimes it still puzzled him why Alexandros hadn't tested his paternity the moment Galen had been born, but Alexandros had always been a proud man. Perhaps he'd never wanted anyone to know that he'd been cuckolded.

Or perhaps he just wanted a reason for his hate. Perhaps you were really his son after all, and he hated you anyway...

Galen stopped that thought dead in its tracks. No, he *wasn't* Alexandros's son. It was the only logical reason for his father's loathing.

Regardless, he didn't want Solace to feel unwanted the way he had, because it wasn't her fault. Just as it hadn't been his fault his mother had found pleasure with someone else. His parents' disastrous marriage wasn't something he wanted to repeat himself. Not when he knew intimately how it could affect a child.

As he looked at her, at the anger in her eyes and the fear beneath it, he realised that her feelings about this mattered very much. She mattered. She was Leo's mother and the woman he'd chosen to be his queen and he wouldn't have her feeling somehow less due to something that had happened in her past. Because whatever it had been, she hadn't let it crush her. He'd genuinely never seen anyone so strong.

'Listen to me,' he said, and it was a command, with all the weight of his authority. 'You are the woman who left behind everything she knew to blackmail a king for the sake of her child.'

'I was naive. I should have—'

'Yes, you were naive. But you were also brave and fierce and resourceful.'

'I gave away my child!' Her voice shook, real distress in her eyes. 'My own mother gave me away without a thought and I just did the same thing. What kind of mother does that? What kind of person does—?'

Galen lowered his head and stopped her words with his mouth, a kiss to take away her pain. He could feel her trembling against him, but he didn't move. He let the warmth and weight of his body hold her fast. He remembered how she'd relaxed in his hold that night in the club, when he'd put his hand around her throat, and sure enough, after a long moment, he felt the trembles shaking her lessen gradually, until she was completely relaxed beneath him.

Her mouth grew soft under his and he lifted his head. She'd closed her eyes, her breathing a little too quick.

Of course, that was what scared her, her own self-doubt, and he knew all about that, didn't he?

But she didn't need to doubt herself. She was a testament to her own strength and courage, and she needed to believe that.

'You weren't well,' he said, his voice flat and certain. 'You'd just had a baby that you'd had no idea you were going to have. And you thought that what you were doing was best for him. And when you realised you wanted him back, you went out and did exactly that.' He brushed his mouth across hers in a feather-light kiss. 'You were on your own, with no support. You did the best you could with what you had, and you put him first. Every decision you made was for him. That's the best kind of mother, silver girl. You're a tigress. And a tigress is exactly what a queen should be.'

She let out a long breath, and then, finally, her eyes opened again. 'I don't…' Her voice was soft and hoarse. 'What if you change your mind?'

This was a very real fear, he could see it in her eyes, and it puzzled him, because once he made a decision, he stuck to it. But…perhaps she didn't know that? And perhaps, at some point in her life, someone had changed their mind and it had hurt her?

'I won't change my mind,' he said with utter certainty. 'Kings generally don't. Why would you think I would?'

She stared at him for a long moment, the shifting emotional currents in her eyes unreadable. Then she said softly, 'It doesn't matter. Not now.'

'Solace—'

But this time it was her turn to interrupt. 'Kiss me, Galen.' Her hands lifted to his hair, her touch gentle. 'Make me feel good. Please.'

Her honesty laid him open. How could he refuse? Perhaps he didn't need to know everything now. The rest could wait.

So, he kissed her and then he made them both feel so good they forgot the rest of the world even existed for the rest of the night.

CHAPTER SEVEN

SOLACE SAT ON the hand-knotted silk rug and
stared at the open folder she'd set on the floor
in front of her. There was a neat stack of papers
in the folder, the apparent life story Galen's PR
team had given her that she was supposed to
memorise.

Leo was kicking on a blanket beside her,
the living area full of the happy sounds he was
making.

She'd much rather have been playing with
him, but Galen had been very clear that she
was to know all the facts that were given in
that stack of papers. She was supposed to know
this woman's backstory backwards, so it was
instinctive. So it was hers.

It wasn't hers, of course. It was a lie.

Galen had told her not to worry about her
origins, that his PR department would 'put together' something for her that would explain
where she came from and how they met. How

the news of her apparent death had been a cover for something tragic that had happened in her past, but now she was happy and healthy, and she and Galen were to be married.

He'd said such an elaborate backstory was necessary to spare her and Leo as much of the ensuing media circus as possible, as well as to protect the palace. His office could hardly admit to lying about Leo's mother death and so another explanation needed to be constructed.

Solace accepted that, but she didn't fully buy into it. Galen's commitment to his reputation seemed excessive in her opinion, so she'd busied herself with research on his rule, since now she was going to be his queen.

She hadn't known what to expect, perhaps a distant king, a bit too rigid, a bit too staid, and one out of touch with his subjects, but that wasn't what she'd found.

It was clear his people adored him and what she saw on TV and on the web, at official functions and royal walkabouts, and other events where he met his subjects, was a warm, generous man who greeted his citizens with genuine pleasure.

He took an active role in his parliament too, making sure the direction of his country was about putting his people first. For example, he'd done an immense amount of work tackling the poverty that had become entrenched during his father's rule, though plenty of the ruling classes had been unhappy about it and had made no secret of the fact.

Galen had argued with them and then, when they'd blocked his policies, he'd overruled them entirely, which was something the King of Kalithera could legally do.

She admired that. She liked that he wasn't afraid to fight for people who had no one to fight for themselves. People like her, which meant she knew how much that mattered.

But it did make her wonder why, if his people were that important to him, he'd decided to essentially lie to them.

He's altogether too fascinating.

Solace frowned at the papers in front of her, trying not to pay attention to the complicated tangle of her emotions whenever she thought of him. The intense physical desire and the constant knot of tension she'd always carried around with her relaxing whenever he was near. The curiosity she had about him…

Perhaps agreeing to marry him had been a mistake.

Too late now. Especially now you've told him everything.

She swallowed, remembering that night at the palace a week ago, where she'd lain under the reassuring weight of his body, warm and sated and relaxed in the aftermath of their passion. He'd told her that she could trust him and had given her a vow, the strength of an iron conviction in his blue eyes. She'd believed him. More, she'd *wanted* to trust him, and so she'd told him things she'd never thought she'd reveal to another person, about Leo and giving him up, and how, her own mother uppermost in her thoughts, she was afraid that doing so made her a terrible person.

But there had been no censure in his eyes. No blame. He'd been so very matter of fact about how she'd been unwell and vulnerable, and the blame was his. It had been his responsibility and he'd failed her. Then he'd given her a list of all the reasons why she'd make not only an excellent mother, but an excellent queen.

It wasn't what she was used to. Validation had never featured strongly in her life; she'd had to do it for herself.

Solace shifted a paper, staring sightlessly at the pile, memories of what had happened afterwards replaying in her head.

Of how he'd made her feel as good as she'd asked him to on that couch, and later, he'd gathered her in his lap at the table and fed her titbits while asking her every single detail of her life. And as if a dam had cracked and broken, out

it had all come, the foster system and her cha-
otic childhood bounced from one family to the
next. Her failed schooling and the menial jobs
which were all she could get, and her dreams
of going to university and being a lawyer and
helping kids like she'd once been.

The only thing she'd kept back was about
Katherine and the princess bed because it had
felt like too stupid a thing to mention.

Through it all, Galen had listened attentively
and asked questions, making his genuine interest clear, before telling her she could continue
her education right here in Kalithera. He'd also
pointed out that while she couldn't be a lawyer
as Queen, that didn't mean she couldn't get a
law degree and that her position would enable
her to do more for kids like her than being a
lawyer could.

She hadn't thought of that, and it pleased her
more than she'd expected.

All in all, it had been a magical evening. For
a night she'd felt safe, the low level of stress
and anxiety that were always at a constant hum
in the background quietening completely. That
night she'd slept in his arms, in his bed, and
even though they'd barely slept, she'd still felt
rested the next day. The following morning, he'd
taken her back to the little house by the sea,
where Leo was.

She was to stay there until she was officially announced as his fiancée. He visited when he could, spending time with her and Leo, though he did not touch her again, which confused her. He'd said he wanted to wait until after they were married and that they needed to be discreet. His uncle, apparently, was a stickler for protocol and had taken an interest in Galen's more frequent visits to the house. Galen didn't want him going to the press before their engagement could be made public.

Galen was all about discretion, about how no gossip or scandal could be attached to the throne, though he hadn't been clear why this was important. Perhaps it was supposed to be obvious. Perhaps the reasons for the whole lying about her origins thing was supposed to be obvious too.

She didn't like it. Just as she didn't like the way Galen seemed to avoid questions about himself. She'd asked him a few times about his life and his background, what it was like growing up a prince. But he always seemed to evade answering. He'd distract her by talking about Leo, or about some aspect of protocol, or their future as the Kalitheran royal family. And his evasions always worked, because having a family of her own was a dream she'd never let herself have, and the thought of having a family with him seemed more and more attractive.

What about love?

The thought made Solace frown. Love had never been part of her childhood growing up and she'd never seen any evidence of it in the families she'd been placed with. Those families had all been dysfunctional in some way, love seeming to be given and withheld randomly from her perspective.

Having Leo had changed her thoughts on that, though, since she loved Leo regardless of what he did. She'd love him fiercely and without reservation until the day she died, but that was because he was her child. She couldn't imagine loving anyone else like that.

But don't you want to be loved like that?

Solace flicked the cover of the folder over the stack of paper, her heart beating fast. No, absolutely not. How could she? To be loved you had to be someone that someone else wanted, and, even if you were, being yourself wasn't enough for them to keep wanting you. People changed their minds, they just did.

Love wasn't something she could trust, full stop. Besides, she'd grown up fine without it and, also, she had Leo. He was all she needed.

'Solace?' The voice was deep and very familiar.

She looked up and saw Galen standing in the doorway. He was beautiful today, as he was every day she saw him, dressed in a perfectly tailored dark charcoal suit and crisp white cotton business shirt, and her heart gave a funny little leap in her chest.

She smiled, getting quickly to her feet and taking a few steps towards him before she realised what she was doing and stopped. 'Galen,' she said breathlessly, conscious of how much lighter the room seemed now he was here and how much her hands itched to touch him. 'I wasn't expecting you today.' There was an odd ache behind her breastbone, a yearning almost. She didn't understand it.

'I know. I had some time free this afternoon and thought I'd come and visit.' If he'd noticed her breathlessness, he gave no sign, strolling over to where his son lay on the blanket and bending to pick him up. Leo squealed with delighted laughter as Galen tossed him playfully up in the air a couple of times before settling him in the crook of his elbow.

Leo loved being with his father and it was clear from the brilliant smile on Galen's face that he loved being with his son.

But she knew that already. All the times Galen had visited, he'd attended to his son's needs, whatever they were, without hesitation and with absolute authority, whether it was feeding him, changing him, playing with him, or putting him down to sleep.

It made her heart melt to see them together, and as she looked at him now, smiling down at Leo, a tiny part of her couldn't help imagining what it would be like to have him look at her that way.

He never will. Why would he? Why would anyone?

Yet as soon as the thought had entered her head, Galen looked up and smiled, and her heart clenched tight as if he'd put his fingers around it and squeezed. 'I'm also here because I need to talk to you.'

Despite his smile, Solace tensed. The sensation, which for years had been second nature due to the precarious nature of her life, felt foreign now and even more unpleasant for it.

You're becoming too used to the good life. It'll all come crashing down at some stage and you know it.

No, he'd promised that he wasn't going to change his mind, that she could trust him, and he'd meant it. And so far, he hadn't done anything to betray her trust. He hadn't broken his word and sent her away, hadn't forbidden her to see Leo. Hadn't told her he didn't want to marry her after all.

'Oh?' She tried to sound casual. 'What things?'

Something in her tone must have given her away, because he frowned slightly. 'Don't look so worried,' he said. 'It's nothing.'

'I'm not worried,' she responded automatically.

He gave her a dubious look, then turned his attention to his son, rubbing his little tummy to make him giggle, before putting him back down on the blanket.

Straightening to his full height, Galen gave her an assessing look. 'I haven't changed my mind. If that's what's concerning you.'

Solace could feel a blush threatening, which was annoying. She wasn't especially comfortable with him knowing her well enough to be able to tell what she was thinking. It was a new experience for her, and she wasn't sure she liked it. 'I wasn't thinking that,' she said with some dignity.

The look in his blue gaze made it clear that he knew exactly how much of a liar she was, but, strangely, he didn't press her the way he normally did. Instead, he put his hand in the pocket of his trousers and brought out a small velvet box. 'I came here to give you this.'

She stared at the box, her heart giving another jolt. It looked like a ring box. 'I—'

'But before I give it to you, I need to know why you were lying to me just now.'

Okay, so she hadn't escaped after all. *Now* he was going to press her.

Solace forced her gaze from the box to his face. 'Only if you tell me why you felt the need to lie about my background.'

An expression she didn't understand flickered briefly over his perfect features and then was gone. 'It's to protect you from any unwanted attention, I told you. And to protect Leo too. The press can be persistent.'

'You told me my background didn't matter,' she pointed out.

'And it doesn't.'

'Yet you want to lie to your people about where I came from? With that nonsense cover story?'

The lines of his face hardened. 'You have a problem with it?'

'I have a problem with lying in general.' She hesitated. 'If you're so obsessed with not having any gossip or scandal attached to the throne, then why not just tell the truth? Or were you lying when you said my background didn't matter?'

'To be clear, *I* don't care about your background.' His gaze was now distinctly chilly. 'But the media will. The Kings of Kalithera marry aristocracy, it's traditional, plus I've a certain reputation to live up to, a reputation I've had to work at building. What do you think the media will do if they discover that the heir to the throne is the product of a one-night stand?'

'Why is your reputation so important though?'

He was silent, then after a moment said, 'Years ago, at Oxford, I didn't exactly cover myself in glory. I preferred partying to studying, drank too much, had many…liaisons. The media were all over it and the people here were less than impressed. They weren't supportive of me being King and I couldn't blame them. I've worked hard to show them those years are behind me, and I don't want them to think I'm backsliding now.'

She hadn't known that. She hadn't known anything about his past, but this put his reluctance to court media attention into context.

'Okay,' she said slowly. 'But you didn't seem to mind a media firestorm when I threatened to upload my pictures on the Internet. So, why are things different now?'

'Because I'm going to marry you.' There was a faint edge to his voice. 'You'll be bound to the same rules I am, since any scandal attached to your name will then reflect on me.'

'Yes, but it's been years since you were at Oxford, Galen. And your people love you. Why would you care about that now?' Pushing this would no doubt end up making things worse with him, but she couldn't let it go. If this was going to be an issue at some point in the future, she had to know now. 'And what if people find out about me anyway? You can't hide everything for ever. Surely if it got out that you lied about me, that would cause an even bigger scandal?'

'Oh, you can hide a great many things and for years, believe me.' His cool blue eyes were sharp. 'Are you worried about it getting out? Because I can assure you, it won't. The cover story my team put together for you is specifically designed to generate very limited interest. Enough to explain your miraculous reappearance from the dead, but not enough for anyone to investigate further.'

There it was again, that strangely 'off' feeling. As if he wasn't quite telling her the truth. Because maybe his people hadn't wanted him on the throne before, yet they certainly did now. He'd proved himself, surely? After over a decade on the throne?

She shook her head. 'I still don't understand. Do you not trust your people, Galen? Is that why you feel the need to lie to them?'

'I've told you why. I don't need to explain further.' His expression had become icy and hard; he looked every inch the proper king he was supposed to be. Very much *not* the man who'd taken her hands on the night of the ball, the man who'd seduced her thoroughly in the back seat of a limo, who'd pinned her beneath him only the week before. It was as if that man didn't exist.

But he did exist, didn't he? Behind those icy blue eyes and his cool and contained front, there was a different man, a passionate man. A man he was hiding from her, she was sure of it. She just didn't know why.

Solace came over to him and looked up into his perfect face. 'There's something you're not telling me, Galen? What is it?'

'Nothing that concerns you.' He seemed like a stranger now, as if the warm, passionate man she'd known didn't exist. 'And I suggest you leave the subject alone in future.'

Her chest ached and she realised with a kind of shock that it hurt he wouldn't tell her what the issue was. Almost as if she wanted him to trust her just as much as she wanted to trust him.

Have you ever thought that he might not trust you? Trust is a two-way street, remember?

Except she hadn't remembered. For too long her life had been only about survival, having to focus solely on her own needs, because who else would? Having her son to care for felt like a natural extension of that, but Galen?

He wasn't a child, but a man with thoughts and feelings of his own. Another person. A person she wanted to trust, but of course that went both ways.

Do you want him to trust you?

She looked up into those cold blue eyes. A mask he wore, she knew, a front. But there was a man behind that front, a man she wanted very much to know if only he'd let her. And yes, she did want him to trust her.

'I'm going to marry you, Galen,' she said with some determination. 'And while it's true that I don't know much about marriage, I do know that any relationship has to start with trust. You told me I could trust you. So how about you do me the same courtesy?'

His expression didn't change. 'The subject is off-limits, Solace.'

If he thought that was going to put her off, he had no idea who he was dealing with. 'I see, so is that the marriage we're going to have? You dictating what we can and cannot talk about? And me meekly accepting it?' She lifted her chin. 'What kind of example does that set for our son? What kind of dysfunction will that lead to? Because, believe me, I've seen dysfunctional families. I've lived in them. And I won't have

that kind of life for Leo. I won't.' She let him see her certainty, just so he knew what he was dealing with. 'So, if that's the kind of path you want to head down, then I'm telling you now that I won't marry you.'

At first Galen was conscious of nothing but shock. Then a wild fury burst up inside him that seemed totally out of proportion with a mere refusal.

She could *not* refuse him now. She'd agreed to the marriage, and he'd swung his whole PR team into action to put together a decent story of her origins and their love affair for the media. Enough to make sure Kostas didn't start making any trouble.

He'd started looking at his diary for possible wedding dates—asap of course—and had already postponed a visit to Isavere to see Augustine and Khalil, since Augustine was playing host that month. Both his friends had demanded an explanation, but he'd been vague. He hadn't wanted to tell them about Solace just yet. What he wanted, though, was a honeymoon, because he'd restrained himself from taking her for the past week and he was so hungry for her he could barely think.

Perhaps that had been a mistake. Perhaps he shouldn't have kept his distance. Part of it had

been wanting to make sure Kostas didn't start paying too much attention to his visits to the little house where Leo was, and wondering why he was going more than usual and staying for longer. And part of it was wanting to test himself. It wouldn't be necessary, not once they were married, but the challenge would do him good. Because marrying her didn't change the fundamental problem: he wore a crown that might not be his and his past was still an issue while his uncle remained a threat.

He'd also thought she'd need some time to adjust.

Except he hadn't wanted her to adjust so far that she'd changed her mind about marrying him after all.

Trust. Why was she talking about that? She'd given him hers that night in the palace and he hadn't betrayed it. He never would. But surely she couldn't expect him to tell her everything? He couldn't tell her his secret. Even one other person was one person too many, and, when it was his country's safety at stake, he couldn't be too careful.

'No,' he said, iron hard, trying to crush the possessive fury that threatened to strangle him. 'You cannot refuse. You will be marrying me and that is final.'

But she kept shaking her head. 'You can't make me, Galen.'

'I can make you do anything I please,' he snapped, before he could think better of it. 'I'm the King.'

'Really?' she snapped back, grey eyes going silver with annoyance. 'I would never have guessed.'

For a moment anger burned in the air between them, made even worse by the seething sexual chemistry that the past week of abstinence had only built to fever pitch.

She looked stunning today in her casual, light blue skirt, and plain white T-shirt. Pretty and virginal and delicious, making him want to chase her, tear those clothes from her and take her on the floor. Uncover the passion that lurked just under the surface of her skin. That was what he wanted, not her naming all those doubts he'd firmly shoved to the back of his mind.

But she wasn't wrong about marriage or setting examples, and he knew all about that. He'd never witnessed Alexandros's marriage to his mother, but he could guess.

Once he'd asked Alexandros about his mother, but his father had cuffed him and told him never to speak her name in his presence again. Galen had only learned about her from his nannies, and they'd told him that Queen Katerina had been too young, too wild and too passionate for Alexandros, and he'd been too cold and proud for her. It hadn't been a love match. What it had been was a disaster from start to finish, they'd said.

Galen didn't want a marriage like that.

Dysfunctional, Solace had said, and she wasn't wrong. His family—though could he even call one father who'd loathed him a family?—had been extremely dysfunctional.

Is that what you want for Leo?

No, of course it wasn't what he wanted for Leo. But while he'd been able to mention having to rebuild his reputation after his time at Oxford, he hadn't been able to tell her the real truth. He couldn't tell a woman who wanted only safety and stability how precarious his throne was, and how all it would take was one test to bring it down.

You are so certain of what that test will say.

Yes, he was certain. The answer lay in the fury he felt hammering away inside him, in the insatiable need for her that pulsed in his blood. All the base, toxic emotions, anger and jealousy and lust. The emotions that his father had hated, that Galen had tried so hard to get rid of. And all because he'd hoped for one kind word, one smile. One sign that Alexandros hadn't really hated him as much as Galen had feared he did.

But he'd never got that sign and he knew why: he was never Alexandros's son.

But what if you are? What if you're his biological son and he hated you anyway?

No, Galen didn't believe that. He couldn't. Alexandros was all ice, while Galen seemed to be only fire. Plus, his father had made it sound so easy, all the things Galen had to do, all the rules he had to obey. Yet none of it had been easy and he'd never seemed to do it right. 'One would think you were someone else's child,' Alexandros had told him coldly once, after he'd got the line of kings wrong, 'not mine.'

Galen turned away before he said something he'd regret. Leo was fussing, picking up on his parents' tension, so Galen bent and scooped him up, shamelessly using him as a distraction. 'Leo's tired,' he said flatly. 'I'll put him down.'

'He's not quite—'

'I know his schedule.' He was already heading for the door. 'I know what he needs.'

He looked down at his son as he stalked upstairs. All of this was for Leo, that was what he had to remember. Yes, he had to protect his country from Kostas, but Leo was the future.

And a legacy of lies that he'll be forced to continue when he grows up.

Ice settled inside him. What a throne he would leave his son... Mistake upon mistake, lie upon lie, and Leo would have to carry the burden, despite none of it being his fault. But what else could Galen do? The truth would expose Kalithera to Kostas and he wasn't prepared to risk that.

You could tell her. It's not a solution, but at least you won't be bearing this alone.

No, he couldn't share this. It wasn't a burden he'd ever sought, but it was his, nonetheless. She'd been through too much. He couldn't ask her to carry this too.

She is strong, though, you know her strength. And she deserves to know what's at stake.

Taking Leo into his bedroom, Galen prepared him for a nap, laying him down in his cot. Then he stood there a moment, stroking his son's downy forehead a couple of times to settle him.

Perhaps she did deserve to know. So many people had let her down in her life and she had reason to question him. And he couldn't in good conscience keep refusing to answer, not if he wanted their marriage to be successful. He'd just have to consider what answer he could give, because the bare truth wasn't it.

Leo was blinking sleepily and looking as if he was ready for his nap, so Galen turned silently and went out, stalking down the hall and down the stairs, trying to wrestle his recalcitrant emotions into submission before he saw her again.

Yet the moment he stepped back into the living area and saw her standing by the window, the sun shining on her pale hair, his desire and his anger and his possessiveness roared back into life.

He didn't know what it was about her that made him feel this way. It was more than a physical response and it always had been, and whether it was her strength or her passion, or courage, or even the way she relaxed in his hold, trusting him completely, he didn't know. What he was sure was that he felt it and it seemed that no amount of trying to control it worked.

He shoved his hands into his pockets to keep them occupied, his fingers closing automatically around the box that contained the Star of Kalithera, the diamond ring that had graced the finger of many a Kalitheran queen.

Solace had drawn herself up, her chin lifted, looking as if she were Queen already.

'You're right, I'm not telling you everything,' he said, carrying on their conversation as if he hadn't left the room. 'But it's a secret that has the highest of stakes and it affects the throne. It affects Kalithera. It affects our son. And the fewer people who know about it, the better.'

There, that was as much as he was prepared to give her.

'But I'm our son's mother, in case you'd forgotten, and you can't tell me?' She folded her arms, her grey eyes uncomfortably direct. 'I gave you my trust, Galen. Why can't you give me yours?'

Galen gritted his teeth, the edges of the ring box digging into his hand. 'I have. But this is a secret that threatens national security. I don't know what more I can say.'

'You could be honest with me,' she said in the same relentless tone. 'And I'm not talking about whatever your secret is. I'm talking about all the other things you avoid. You know everything about me, Galen. Everything. I didn't want to tell you about my postnatal depression, but I did. I didn't want to tell you about any of the other things either, how I wanted to be a lawyer, all those pipe dreams I had. Yet I did.' The silver in her eyes glittered. 'But I know nothing about you, except you were once a hell-raiser at university.'

'You know about me,' he argued. 'Everything you could want to know is on the Web—'

'I know all about the King. But nothing about the man.'

He didn't want to talk about it. He didn't want to go into his cold, lonely childhood and all the things he'd done wrong that his father had never let him forget. Little things that had become big things, because the older he'd got, the more he'd realised that nothing he did would ever change Alexandros's opinion of him.

So, whatever he'd been told to do, he'd done the opposite, until Alexandros, disgusted with him, had sent him to Oxford. A mistake. Because there he'd found like minds in Augustine and Khalil, and there he'd allowed his anger and pain free rein in the form of drunken parties that had turned into orgies, endless nights in the clubs in London, too much alcohol and too much of other things. Getting into trouble with the police on the odd occasion, because he just hadn't been able to stop himself from pushing all the boundaries. And the more the press had made sensations out of everything the 'Wicked Princes' had done, the more he'd wanted to do them.

He'd been a selfish young man back then. Everything he'd done in a mindless knee-jerk reaction to Alexandros's active loathing. Goading him, pushing him, seeing how far he could take it before Alexandros finally repudiated him.

And then that party at one of his friends' houses in London had happened. There had been too much alcohol involved, too many party drugs, and when the police had finally broken it up, they'd discovered a whole lot of under-age girls. The girls hadn't been invited, they'd sneaked in, and Galen hadn't known how old they were at the time. He hadn't had anything to do with them, but, as far as the press went, it had been the story of the year.

Alexandros's stroke had had nothing to with the media storm that had broken afterwards, or at least that was what the doctors had told Galen, but that had been the last straw as far as Alexandros had been concerned.

'You are not my son,' he'd said. 'And I will not have you on the throne. You are unfit to be King and you always have been.'

No, he did not want to tell Solace that. Not any of it.

Yet he had to give her something. He'd promised her a life, and he wanted her in his bed. He wanted her at his side as Leo's mother. She had to marry him and if she was going to then he wanted her to be happy. He did not want to re-peat his parents' marriage.

'Very well,' he said flatly. 'My mother died when I was born, and my father was a cold and distant man. My childhood was unpleasant—I was rather a handful, and he didn't know how to deal with me, so when he sent me away to Oxford, it was a relief. I was called back to Ka-lithera after he had a stroke and when he died soon after, I ascended the throne. Is that what you wanted to know?'

She frowned, her silver gaze searching. 'What do you mean "unpleasant"?'

Galen found he was squeezing the ring box even tighter, a familiar hot fury coiling in his gut. A fury he'd been trying to deny for years without success, which didn't make sense. It had been years—*years*—since Alexandros had died and he had proved himself. He should not still be so angry with him.

'Alexandros was very strict,' he said. 'There was a level of behaviour expected and he punished me when I didn't meet those expectations. And I didn't meet those expectations very often. I was…rebellious and headstrong, and he was… exacting. He…did not like me.'

A look of fleeting shock passed over Solace's face and she took a step towards him, then stopped. 'But he was your father. Why would he not like you?'

He gave a short laugh. 'Because nothing I did was good enough for him, nothing was right. And he always made it very clear that I wasn't the son he wanted.' The shock had gone from her expression now, leaving behind it a concern that felt like a needle sliding beneath his skin. 'It was years ago,' he went on roughly. 'There's no need to look at me like that. It wasn't as if I was starving on the streets.'

She took another step towards him. 'It doesn't matter. That's a terrible way to handle a child. And I should know. I had plenty of foster parents who treated me that way.' She gave him another of those direct, searching looks. 'Why did he do that to you? Who did he want you to be?'

He couldn't tell her the truth. That it didn't matter that Galen might actually be his son, what Alexandros wanted was for Galen not to exist.

'I don't know. Someone else.'

'But—' Solace began.

But nothing. He was done with this conversation. The more they talked about himself, the closer they got to the truth and he wasn't going to tell her. He couldn't.

'I think that's enough about me for one day.' He pulled out the ring box once again. 'Here. I need to give you this.'

But she didn't look at the box. She kept her direct grey gaze on him instead. 'You're very angry with him, aren't you?'

He could feel a muscle twitch in his jaw. 'My father is dead. I am his son, and I am the King now.' He flicked open the box. 'Hold out your hand.'

She didn't move. 'No.'

His impatience rose and along with it, his frustration. 'Your hand, Solace.'

The look in her eyes was sharp as a blade and there was no escape. 'You told me that I could trust you and yet you won't trust me.'

'It is not a matter of trust. I can't—'

'Then what kind of future can we have? What kind of future are we going to give our son?'

She was so definite. So certain. The only woman who'd ever confronted him like this— the only *person*. And he could feel his grip on his temper loosening, the hot, suffocating emotions that had always lurked too close to the surface all boiling up.

He was so tired of having to keep a grip on them. So tired of lying, of having to protect a secret that wasn't even his. So tired of trying to be better than a man who hated him and who hadn't wanted him on the throne.

So tired of trying to put his past behind him in order to be a good king.

There was only one way to deal with his anger and that was to turn it into pleasure and let it burn the way he'd so often done at Oxford. But it wasn't some random woman he wanted to burn with him, he wanted Solace.

He'd *always* wanted her. Even when he hadn't known anything about her, not even her name, he'd wanted her. Those silvery eyes behind the mask, the way she'd looked at him, not know-ing he was a king. The way she'd wanted him just as badly as he'd wanted her…

She'd haunted his dreams for over a year and he'd thought at first it was just physical. But it wasn't. It never had been.

She'd seen something in him that no one else did, maybe the hot-headed, restless, stubborn boy he'd once been, and she'd matched him.

She was as passionate and stubborn as he was, which would have made it a marriage made in heaven if her blunt honesty hadn't cut through the web of lies he'd surrounded himself with.

He wanted to close the space between them, wanted to hold her down and restrain her, feel her melt against him in total acceptance, be-cause that was what she'd always given him. She surrendered to him as he was, not a king, but a man.

But there was no surrender in her now.

He could make her, render her incoherent with pleasure. But it wouldn't mean anything if he had to take it from her. She had to give him her surrender willingly.

Abruptly the expression on her face changed, and she was the one coming to him, crossing the space between them, the look in her eyes full of a compassion he'd never seen before.

She lifted her hands and laid them on his

chest, her silver eyes glittering as she looked up at him. 'I'm sorry,' she said. 'I don't want to force anything from you. You don't have to tell me if you don't want to.'

The apology went through him like a sword. He was used to digging in, to being stubborn, to resisting, and, used to the fight, he stared down at her, for a second lost.

But he saw the flames in her eyes suddenly leap, the heat between them building, and he didn't think.

He lifted his hands, plunged his fingers into her hair and took her mouth as if it were water and he were a man dying of thirst.

CHAPTER EIGHT

SOLACE HAD TAKEN one look at the rigid lines of Galen's face and had known that one of them had to give in. At least in this moment. Because whatever secret he was keeping it had clearly trapped him and was torturing him.

There had been fury in his eyes and yet he'd been so still, as if frozen, rigid as a board while a volcano of emotion erupted behind his eyes. And all she'd been able to think about was how, if she wanted his trust, forcing him to give her something he'd told her he couldn't wasn't the way to go about it.

Trust was slow to earn, and she knew that all too well. He'd taken some steps to building it with her, but she needed to take some steps too. It wasn't all on him, no matter what had happened with Leo, and it couldn't be, not if she wanted this marriage to work.

Plus, while fighting him was exhilarating, that couldn't be the whole of their relationship.

Someone had to take the first step towards a compromise, and it was clear to her that he either wouldn't or couldn't. Whatever this secret was, keeping it was hurting him, she could see it in his eyes, and it wasn't until this minute that she realised she didn't like that. His pain mattered to her. In fact, it made her hurt too.

His father and his 'unpleasant' childhood, for example. Because she knew what it felt like. His upbringing might have been a thousand times more privileged than hers, but that didn't make it a happy one. And it was clear it still affected him on some deep level.

He'd always been kind to her, right from that first encounter, and, despite the pain involved with Leo being taken from her, she couldn't keep throwing that in his face. They had to move on from it somehow, and he was trying to make it right. He deserved her kindness as much as she deserved his.

So, she'd crossed the gap between them and laid her hands against his chest, told him she'd never force anything from him that he didn't want to give, and in that instant she'd seen shock leap in his eyes, then a wild, rushing heat.

Then he was kissing her, his mouth on hers hot and demanding and feverish, and she could taste the need in him. Some part of her recognised it. The need for connection, for closeness, and she understood. His childhood sounded as if it had been as barren as hers, so of course that was what he wanted.

But he'd done so much for her already and it was time for her to reciprocate.

Solace tore her mouth from his and pushed him back over to the couch. He went without resistance, dropping down on it. Then she went to her knees in front of him, leaning forward between his powerful thighs, reaching for the buttons of his suit trousers.

His fingers wove their way through her hair. 'I promised myself I wouldn't touch you,' he murmured. 'I promised myself I'd be good.'

'You don't have to be good.' She undid the zip of his trousers, her fingers already shaking as blind need began to rise. 'I want to do something for you, Galen. You've done so much for me, now it's my turn.'

His grip in her hair tightened. 'But this marriage, Solace? What about that?'

It had always been something of a bluff. She'd never been going to refuse, not when it would leave her in the same position, having to choose between staying for her son and leaving for herself. And she'd have to leave, because she couldn't take Leo away from Galen. Not only when it would condemn Leo to the kind of life she'd had herself, but also it would hurt Galen immeasurably.

She couldn't do that. Just as she couldn't walk away from him. And it wasn't to do with his power or the fact that he was a king or because of their chemistry. It wasn't about the kind of life he could give her. It wasn't even because he was Leo's father.

It was him. She wanted to stay with him because when she was in his arms, she felt safe. When he looked at her, she felt as if she was worth something for the first time in her life. And when she spoke, he listened. She wasn't invisible with him.

With him she was seen.

'I'll marry you, Galen,' she said, then reached inside his trousers and found him, hard and ready and hot in her hands.

His body was tense, all his muscles rigid, and he murmured something sharp and bitten off as she slowly drew him out. His skin was smooth and velvety, and her mouth watered as she leaned forward to taste him.

He tightened his fingers convulsively as she licked him, tracing the long, hard line of his sex with her tongue. Then he growled her name as she took him into her mouth, taking him deep. His hands firmed and she let him guide her, because this was for him, after all, and she wanted to give him everything she could.

She let him direct her, sucking him hard and then softer, slower, her own fingers digging into his rock-hard thighs, dizzy and drunk on the taste of him.

She didn't stop. She took him to the edge and when the climax hit him, it came hard and fast, his grip on her hair painful, his low, masculine growls of satisfaction making her own need build.

But she didn't care about herself, not this time, because there was so much satisfaction in giving him what he needed. She hadn't realised until now how good that would feel. So much of the time she had to put her own needs first, but taking care of his, taking care of him, satisfied something deep in her soul she hadn't realised was there.

After a moment, Galen loosened his fingers in her hair and pulled her up into his lap, holding her with her head against his broad chest, and for a while they sat like that, content in the silence.

Then Galen said, his voice a low rumble in her ear, 'Nine months before I was born, my mother had one night with one of the palace staff. She and my father were trying for an heir at the time.'

Solace went very still, staring at the white cotton of his shirt.

'She died a few days after I was born due to complications from the birth. There were rumours about the affair, but no one knew for certain. No one except my father. A simple paternity test would have solved the issue of who my actual father was, but Alexandros was a proud man. He couldn't stand the thought of anyone knowing his wife had been unfaithful, and he needed an heir, so he claimed me as his anyway.'

He was very warm, the tension gone from his muscles, an arm around her waist. She could hear the beat of his heart. It was fast.

So…what did all of this mean?

'Alexandros never had me tested,' Galen went on. 'He didn't tell me that there was a possibility he wasn't my father until I was called back from Oxford after his stroke. That's when he… disowned me. He told me about my mother and her affair, that it had always been clear to him that I wasn't his son and my behaviour at Oxford proved it. Then he told me he was going to pass the crown on to my uncle, Kostas.'

Shock rippled through her, but she stayed silent. It was clear he still had things to say.

'Kostas never cared about the people of this country. It was all about big business and making the rich richer while making the poor even poorer. I couldn't allow that to happen. I couldn't allow him to rule and so when Alexandros died before he could formally change the succession, I took the throne even though it might not be mine by right.' He paused. 'Everyone assumed I was the true heir and so I let them keep on believing that in order to protect Kalithera. Kostas doesn't know the truth but Alexandros must have let slip something because he'd always been deeply suspicious of me. I cannot afford to give him any reason to question me or my rule, especially not considering my past, because if I do, if I have to take that test and it finds I'm not Alexandros's son, then the throne will pass to him.'

Slowly Solace shifted her head and looked up at him. 'But you don't know for sure that you're not Alexandros's son?'

Galen's deep blue eyes were impenetrable. 'No. But if I'm not, I'll have to abdicate in favour of Kostas. He's already tried to block a number of the policies I've put in place to help tackle the poverty we've had here, and he's made no secret of the fact he wants to turn Kalithera into a tax haven.' His expression hardened. 'I won't have it. I won't allow my country to be turned over to big business and criminals, and if I have to lie in order to protect it, I will.'

Anger glittered in his eyes now, the strength of his conviction finding an echo inside her too. She knew what it was to fight for something, to do anything you could to protect the things that mattered, that you cared about.

But still, that this would be the secret he was hiding had never even occurred to her, and she could see now why he hadn't wanted to tell her. This affected not only the stability of his throne, but his entire country.

She studied his beautiful face. 'You don't have to take the test, surely?'

His expression betrayed nothing. 'No, I don't. But if questions about my paternity were asked and I refused to take a test, it would create doubt in people's minds. There would be questions about my right to the throne, especially considering my past, and Kostas would take advantage of that. And of course, if they'd question me, they'd definitely question Leo.'

The shock spread out, ice water in her veins.

Of course. This affected Leo too.

'Galen—'

'That is why I cannot have any press looking too closely at me. It's not just about what happened in Oxford, it's about Kostas too. He's tried to use my past against me before, to discredit my suitability to rule, and I cannot give him any more ammunition. That's why I had to bring Leo here. I cannot have a son of mine, my DNA, living anywhere but with me. I have to go on as if I was Alexandros's son, even if I'm not, because that's the only way I can protect this country and the people in it.'

She put a hand on the cotton of his shirt, feeling the warmth of his hard chest beneath it. 'But you might actually be his son, in which case none of this is necessary.'

His expression hardened. 'But I might not. In which case the throne goes to Kostas and everything I've tried to do for my people will be undone.'

It was a terrible problem, she could see that now. For anyone else, a simple test would have cleared up any questions, but not in this instance. A simple test would certainly give answers, but it also might lose him everything. Of course, he couldn't take it.

'You can't let that happen, can you?' she murmured, looking up into his face. 'That's why you have to lie about me?'

'I've never wanted to lie, believe me,' he said bleakly. 'But for the past ten years it's been more a lie of omission than anything else, at least, until…' He stopped.

But she didn't need him to go on. She knew already what he was going to say.

Until Leo had been born. Until she'd turned up, complicating everything.

Pain twisted in her gut, her throat closing. 'Oh, God. Leo and I must—'

'No,' he interrupted, unexpectedly fierce. 'I will never regret Leo. *Never.* And you...' His blue gaze burned. 'I will never regret you, either.'

The pain eased, but the lump in her throat didn't go away, no matter how many times she swallowed. 'But you have to lie to your people for me.'

Galen touched her cheek gently, but the intensity in his gaze didn't falter. 'You are worth every lie I have to tell. Every single one.'

Her chest ached with a sudden tightness, and she had to look away from the intensity in his eyes, concentrating instead on her thumb moving across the fine cotton of his shirt, stroking him. 'You don't think you're Alexandros's son, do you?' It seemed obvious since if he truly believed he was, then he wouldn't have gone to all this trouble to play games with the truth. And he would have taken that test.

He didn't even hesitate. 'No. I do not.'

'Can I ask why?'

He didn't answer immediately, reaching down for her hand where it lay on his chest and taking it in his. 'Alexandros didn't just not like me, he hated me. I could see it in his eyes every time he looked at me. And just in case I didn't understand why, he told me before he died that I was no son of his.' Galen paused a moment. 'That trouble I had at Oxford was a party I attended that ended up in the press. There was alcohol, party drugs, plus some under-aged girls somehow got in, and the fact that I was there was made into a big deal. Alexandros was furious and told me that was the last straw, that no son of his would ever have been involved in that.' Galen shook his head. 'He said I'd never make a good king, that I was unfit for it, which is why he was going to pass the crown to Kostas.'

Solace felt something inside her shift and tighten at the echo of pain she could hear beneath the words. 'You wanted to be his son?'

A flicker of anger crossed his face. 'Once, I did. Once, I wanted to follow in his footsteps. And I'd have done anything to get him to look at me with kindness, just once, but...' Galen glanced at her. 'There are only so many times you can try pleasing someone determined to resent your very existence. So, no. No, I didn't want to be his son.' A muscle flicked in his hard jaw. 'Sometimes I think it wasn't my behaviour he wanted to correct, but my very existence.'

Her throat constricted with a terrible sympathy. 'It's not your fault, Galen. You do know that, don't you? It wasn't fair for him to take it out on you. You can't take responsibility for the mistakes your parents made.'

His gaze met hers. 'And yet that is all I'm doing now, is it not? I didn't want the crown in the end. I wanted him to disown me, I wanted him to admit that he hated me, that he'd never wanted me, and that's exactly what he did.' Galen let out a breath. 'Sometimes I wonder if I only took the crown to spite him. Because he was so desperate for me not to have it.'

Her hand in his felt warm and so did he, and she wished she could give him the same kind of reassurance that he gave her. 'No,' she said quietly. 'That's not why you took it. You took it because you wanted to protect your country and do right by its people. That's what being a good king is.'

There were shadows in his eyes. 'But I'm not a good king, Solace. I'm not…suited for it. I did everything I could to throw the crown in my father's face and when he disowned me, I instantly took it back.'

'Yes. To save your country.'

'Or was it more to spite my father? Perhaps that I could do a better job than my uncle is just another lie I tell myself.'

She stared at him. 'Do you really believe that?'

He said nothing, but he didn't need to. She could see the truth in his face.

'No,' she said again, more fiercely this time. 'No, it's not true. I did my research about your rule, I saw what kind of king you are. You're compassionate and kind, and you care so much about your people. You want to do the best for them, and you're prepared to fight for them.' She took her hand from his and laid her palm against his cheek, feeling the warmth of his skin. 'Your father was wrong, Galen. You're a good king. You're an excellent king. And the only standards you should be meeting are your own.'

'Solace...'

'Listen to me. I don't know who my father is, or my mother. And I'll never know since they didn't want to be found. So I had to decide who I wanted to be. I think, in the end, all you can do is decide that it doesn't matter what your background is or where you came from. Or who brought you up and how. All that matters are the choices you make, and only you get to decide who you are.' She stroked her thumb across his cheekbone. 'Don't let one man's wrong opinion of you determine who you get to be, Galen. You are more, so much more than that.'

He gave her a long look and didn't speak.

Then slowly, he nodded. 'I shouldn't have told you all of this, you know.'

'So why did you? What changed your mind?'

'You've been so very honest with me and so I wanted to be honest with you.' He caught her hand against his cheek. 'You were right about trust. I want this marriage to work, and we have to start somewhere.'

In spite of herself, Solace's heart gave the oddest leap. She smiled. 'I want it to work too. And speaking of trust, I won't tell anyone else what you told me, Galen. I swear on Leo's life.'

He nodded then opened his hand and bent his head, dropping a kiss into the middle of her palm. 'I know you won't. Now… I'd better do what I came here to do.' Reaching into his trouser pocket, he brought out the ring box and flicked it open. Sitting in it was the largest diamond Solace had ever seen.

Galen took the ring out of the box and slid it gently onto her finger.

It fitted perfectly.

CHAPTER NINE

A WEEK LATER, Galen sat in a chair and watched Solace turn slowly in front of the mirror the designer had brought into the living area, unable to tear his gaze from her.

She wore a gown that had been made for her by one of Kalithera's best designers—Galen was a firm believer in locally made products.

It was strapless, with a fitted silver bodice that then frothed out into a cloud of silver skirts down to the ground. The silk shimmered and the whole thing had been hand-beaded, so the gown sparkled as if it had been dusted with diamonds. It left her shoulders bare, her pale hair falling down her back, and she looked like an angel. She looked like a queen.

It was the gown she'd wear for her formal presentation as his bride, a tradition that all Kalitheran rulers followed when they got engaged.

Galen had been reluctant to give one for himself, considering the stakes, but since it was part of tradition and it would cause more comment if he *didn't* present her, he couldn't afford not to do it. So, he'd ordered the ball to be arranged and quickly.

Their marriage needed to happen as soon as possible since he wanted Solace with him at the palace. But since she hadn't been formally presented yet, her presence would have caused a lot of unwanted gossip and so she had to stay in the little house by the sea with Leo.

He hadn't wanted to tell her the truth about his paternity, yet that day he'd tried to give her his ring, when she'd gone on her knees for him and given him so much pleasure, the words had just spilled out. He'd been carrying them for so long and he was tired of it.

In fact, there were a great many things he was tired of, and even though he'd told himself he didn't want to share the toxic relationship he'd had with his father with her, he'd told her anyway. And once he had, he couldn't remember why *not* doing so had felt so important.

She'd understood too, and after he'd told her he'd felt as if a weight had lifted from him. His burdens had always been heavy ones and he was used it, but it was good to share the load a little.

Afterwards, he'd wondered if she'd see him differently once she knew that his throne might not be his. That she'd view his kingship, too, in a different light, after he'd told her about his father's belief that he was unfit to rule.

Yet she hadn't. She'd laid her hand on his cheek and told him he was a good king, an excellent king even, and there had been conviction in her eyes. As if she believed everything she said.

He hadn't known that was something he'd needed to hear until she'd said it. He hadn't known it would matter to him, but it did. And so did she.

There didn't seem to be much point in testing himself by keeping his distance from her, so he didn't, and those few hours he could spare with her were precious and not just for the pleasure they both took from each other, but also for afterwards, lying in each other's arms and talking. Her telling him about the shock of her pregnancy and those six months where she'd struggled. While he shared his own shock at finding out he had a son. And other things too, plans for their little family and whatever the future might hold.

She was nervous about the ball, though. It put her under pressure, and he was well aware of the fact. He'd drilled her in her backstory personally, making sure she knew it backwards and forwards in the hope it would make her feel more comfortable when the time came. And he'd promised her that he'd be at her side the whole night, especially with Kostas likely to be there. He wouldn't leave her to manage on her own.

He understood her nervousness. She hadn't been brought up for this. It was alien to her, as was Kalithera, its politics and its language. She could get away with not knowing any of that, since he'd kept as much of her own story as he could in the fiction they'd crafted for her, but if there was an error or inconsistency...

The palace would be exposed and potentially the throne along with it.

Solace's grey eyes caught his in the mirror for a second, then she hurriedly looked away, a stain of pink in her cheeks.

Galen sat forward. 'Would you excuse us?' he said to the designer, who inclined her head and vanished through the doorway.

Once she'd gone, Galen rose from the chair and crossed to where Solace stood, coming to stand behind her. 'Do you like the dress? You look unsure.'

She let out a breath. 'No, I love the dress. I just...feel a bit like an imposter in it.'

He met her gaze in the mirror and held it. 'You're beautiful in it. You're a queen.'

The expression on her face eased. 'I had a foster mother once, Katherine, who was going to adopt me and she said that when I was finally her daughter, she'd get me a princess bed.' Solace glanced back at her reflection. 'Except she changed her mind, and I never got that bed. And now look at me.' Her voice had gone husky. 'I never thought...'

That this was a painful memory for her was obvious. That she'd offered it to him without him asking or pressing for more made his breath catch.

This was her trust, he understood, and it was rare and precious, and it made his heart ache.

'You never thought that you were that princess all along, hmm?' He settled his hands on her waist, the beads pressing against his palms. 'And not only a princess, but a queen-in-waiting.'

Her hands came to rest over his, her eyes shimmering with tears. 'It's silly to feel so much about a stupid bed. But to this day I don't know why she changed her mind about the adoption. Whether it was something I did or said... All I remember is that I didn't get the bed.'

It wasn't only about the bed, he could see that. Solace had been promised a mother, being part of a family, and then this Katherine had changed her mind. There must have been some reason for it, and hopefully a good reason, but right now

Galen didn't care what that reason was. Whatever it had been, it had hurt her.

'It would not have been something you did.' He let the conviction ring in his voice the way it had rung in hers a week ago. 'I can guarantee you that right now. Because who wouldn't want you, silver girl?'

A tremulous smile turned her mouth. 'Some people might not.'

'Those people are fools. Also, you don't need Katherine. I'll get you a princess bed. I'll get you as many princess beds as you desire.'

The pain in her eyes faded, to be replaced by something else, something much warmer, the smile losing its tremulousness and deepening. 'I don't need a princess bed, Galen. I don't even need a crown. You make me feel like a queen already.'

His breath caught at that smile, at the look in her eyes, making him feel as if someone had punched him in the stomach.

She feels something for you.

The thought crossed his mind like a comet, trailing flames and sparks, and it shocked him. Because somehow it had never occurred to him that emotions might factor into any of this. His own, certainly not. But hers? He'd had no idea.

It changed things. It changed things completely.

This marriage wasn't based on emotion, but necessity. He hadn't thought about feelings.

Except you feel something for her too, you can't deny it.

Galen let her go and turned away abruptly, unable to bear her gaze. He took a couple of steps towards the door, then stopped. His heart was beating faster than it should and he had the strangest urge to stride back to her, pull her into his arms and keep her there, never let her go.

No, he didn't feel anything for her. Or at least nothing beyond friendship, but her... She felt something for him, and what it was, he wasn't sure, but one thing he did know: he didn't want her to feel it. Because while he could give her a crown and a home, create a safe and stable space for her and their son, if it was love she wanted, he couldn't give her that.

How could he? When he didn't even know what love was? His mother had died having him and his father had hated him from birth. No one had ever shown him, no one had ever taught him.

Perhaps there's a reason for that. And it's not because you were potentially another man's child, but because you're someone no one can love.

Cold seeped through him. All his life, his father's hatred had never wavered and maybe the reason was him. A wrongness in himself, that he'd been born with, that made him impossible to care for.

He'd tried over the years to compensate for it, to learn how to be a decent king, He'd made mistakes—he was even continuing to make them—and perhaps he could even learn to be a decent husband and father. But he had to face the fact that he'd never be able to compensate for that wrongness, that lack of whatever it was that would have made his father love him.

He had no examples to follow, no rules or guidelines to keep him on the right track. And he couldn't afford mistakes, not with Solace and not with his son. He had to be perfect for both of them, because they both deserved perfection.

Except he wasn't perfect. And he'd fail, the way he'd failed with Alexandros. He'd make mistakes and he'd hurt them.

Then she'd finally see that wrongness in you, and then she'll end up hating you too.

The cold turned to ice. He couldn't allow that. He couldn't allow their marriage to turn toxic because of him. It was better she felt nothing for him, because it would turn to hate in the end, and that would hurt not only Solace, but Leo too.

'Galen?' Her voice came from behind him,

soft and puzzled-sounding. 'Is there something wrong?'

Unfair of you to bring her into this mess you created and give her such a heavy burden of responsibility to carry. Especially considering you cannot give her what she so desperately needs.

The ice spread through him, freezing him solid. Because regardless of how she felt about him, Solace herself needed to be loved. No one in her life ever had, and the closest she'd got to having it had been Katherine, who'd changed her mind.

Another impossible situation.

And yes, it was impossible. He'd never been loved himself, he had no idea what it felt like, so how could he give it to her? He'd be condemning her to a loveless marriage, because how could he change his mind and not marry her? Do to her what Katherine had done to her?

He took a breath but it felt as if he couldn't get enough air. It made his chest hurt, as if someone had wrapped barbed wire around it. He didn't want to turn around and meet those sharp grey eyes of hers, the ones that looked deep into his soul. She'd be able to see what was there, or rather the lack of what was there. She'd know. He could pretend with everyone else, but he couldn't pretend with her. That would be one lie too many.

He'd promised he'd marry her, and he couldn't break that promise, not when he'd given his word. He couldn't break that trust. But she had to know that was all she'd ever have from him. Their marriage would be based on mutual respect and the bond they shared as parents, but that bond didn't include love. Maybe it never would.

Galen turned.

She stood in front of the mirror with her back to it, her gaze soft. There was a small crease of concern between her fair brows.

She was so beautiful. Dressed all in silver and looking like spun starlight.

His chest ached, the barbed wire digging in. She was going to make such a wonderful queen. A better queen than he was a king.

His expression must have given him away, because she came over to where he stood, her dress glittering with every step she took. 'Something's wrong.' She stopped in front of him, the crease between her brows deepening. 'What is it?'

She could read him so well, she always had. And he couldn't keep it from her. She'd taught him about honesty and now he had to give it back to her.

'This marriage between us,' he said, keeping

his voice very level and measured. 'It isn't one of the heart. You do understand that, don't you?'

'I'm not quite sure what you mean.'

'I mean, we're not marrying for love.'

'I know.' Expressions flickered across her face, gone so fast he couldn't read any of them, but she clasped her hands, the beginnings of a hopeful smile curving her mouth. 'But... I hope that eventually, given time, we might—'

'No,' he interrupted, the ice inside him creeping into his voice no matter how hard he tried to stop it. 'That's what I'm trying to say, Solace. Love will *never* be part of it.'

For a second there was shock on her face and a bright flare of what could only be anguish in her eyes. Then it was gone, nothing but the guardedness he remembered from when she'd first tried to blackmail him returning. 'Can I ask why?' Her tone gave nothing away.

'Because love was never a part of my life,' he said bluntly. 'I know what it isn't, but I couldn't tell you what it is. And I feel that you should know that before we marry.'

Her chin lifted in that challenging way she had and she gave him a look that was almost regal. 'And why did you feel that I should know that?'

Tension pulled his muscles rigid, and he found himself wishing that he could take her in his arms and kiss her senseless so she wouldn't ask him these questions. So they wouldn't have to have this conversation. But it was too late to take what he'd said back and so he went on, 'Because I want you to be clear what I can and cannot give you. I can promise you the life you always wanted and a crown too, as well as a family. But love will not be a part of it.' He took a silent breath, because he could see only one way out for her. 'I won't break my promise to you. I gave you my word that I wouldn't change my mind, and I haven't. But the choice to go through with this marriage is yours. And if you decide not to, then I understand.'

Solace stared at him, and he couldn't have said what she was thinking. Then, abruptly, anger sharpened in her gaze. 'I see. You haven't got the guts to break it off yourself, so you're going to make me do it?'

This time the shock was his, echoing through him, cold as a north wind, a growing anger coming along behind it. 'No, that's not what I said. I don't want to get out of it.' He took a step towards her. 'I mean to marry you, believe me. But I needed you to know that if you're looking for love from me, you won't get it.'

He stood there radiating tension, looking impossibly gorgeous in dark trousers and a shirt of midnight blue. His eyes, though, had gone dark, the lines of his beautiful face rigid.

She didn't understand why they were having this conversation. His proclamation about love had seemed to come out of the blue. Or perhaps not. She'd told him about Katherine and the princess bed, because the words had just fallen right out of her. It had felt natural to tell him, and when he'd looked at her in the mirror and said that people were fools not to want her and that he'd buy her a princess bed, there had been nothing but conviction in his eyes.

Her heart had tightened in that moment, as if someone had wrapped their fingers around it and squeezed hard, and so she'd told him he made her feel like a queen, because it was the truth. And more than that, she felt like *his* queen.

Yet then he'd pulled away.

She'd been too honest, hadn't she? She'd let her feelings show, feelings that had been building inside her for the past week they'd been together, that had coalesced that moment he'd looked into her eyes in the mirror and told her she was a queen.

She could feel it inside her now, a longing, an ache. And she knew that continuing to argue with him about this was betraying herself even further and that he would know. But suddenly she didn't care.

This marriage with him was something she'd come to want, but not only for Leo. All her life she'd wanted safety and stability, a home, a family, and he was going to give her that. But now, as she looked at him, so impossibly beautiful, the dense blue of his eyes full of shadows, she knew that wasn't enough.

She wanted him. She wanted to love him and be loved by him in return. And she was going to argue for it, because the objections he was giving her didn't make any sense. 'Why not?' she asked.

A muscle flicked in his hard jaw. 'I told you. How can love ever be a part of our marriage when I have no idea what love is?'

'I don't believe that. You think anyone ever loved me growing up? You think any one of those families ever cared about me? No, they didn't. But I know what love is, Galen, because I love our son.' She took a step towards him, wanting him to understand. 'And you can't tell me you don't love him. I see your face when you look at him, when you smile at him. Whether you know it or not, you love him just as much as I do.'

'Is it love, Solace?' His voice was cool. 'Or is it because he's my heir and I'm supposed to feel that way?'

He couldn't possibly think that. *Why* would he think that? He was Leo's father, and she could see the love in his eyes when he held Leo in his arms. He had to feel it just as she did.

Why would he? When he was brought up by a man who hated him?

She'd been brought up by people who hadn't cared about her, too. Except...there had been times where she'd seen moments of caring in a playground, where a mother would comfort a crying child. Or even in the street, a husband pulling his wife in for an embrace and a kiss. Brief moments, enough to wonder what it would be like to have those for herself.

But Galen wouldn't have had those moments, not in the insular world of the palace, with a father who'd never seen him as a son and never treated him like one.

'It's not duty,' she said. 'I'm his mother and I can tell you I don't feel it's duty.'

'Be that as it may, the bond between a child and parent is different.' He seemed to be retreating from her, withdrawing into a distant kind of formality. 'I'm not trying to be cruel, Solace, I hope you know that. I just... I've made so many mistakes with you.' His eyes had darkened into the same midnight as his shirt. 'I don't want to hurt you any more than I have already.'

'You think I'm not hurt now?' Even two weeks ago, she'd never have admitted that. But things were different now and she wanted him to know that this mattered to her.

'I'm sorry.' There was a fine edge of pain in his voice. 'But that's why I had to tell you. Better you know going in exactly what you can expect from me.'

'Which is nothing.' It hurt. It hurt more than she thought possible. Because she hadn't known what she'd wanted until now, not truly. Hadn't known what she craved with every part of her, which was him.

Anguish glittered in his eyes. 'I'm sorry,' he said again. 'I'm trying to do the right thing for you.'

'What if the right thing for me is you loving me?' She couldn't help herself, the words came right out. 'What if the right thing for me is us loving each other?'

'Solace—'

'Don't we deserve that, Galen? We had no one growing up, no one who cared, but now we have each other. We want the same things so why can't we have them? And why can't we give them to our son?'

His eyes were almost black now, as if the shadows were consuming him whole. 'You deserve it, silver girl. And so does Leo, that goes without question. But…it took me years to learn how to be a decent king and I've made so many mistakes. I'm still making them. And it will take me years to learn how to be a decent husband too, if that's even possible. I'll fail you, Solace. At some point I will, and I'll fail Leo too, and I cannot… I just cannot bear that.' He was holding himself so rigidly he looked as if he might shatter at the slightest touch.

She had been angry with him just before, but it had all gone now, leaving behind it an aching sorrow. All those years he'd spent trying to please the one man who should have loved him, who should have encouraged him to be the passionate, caring, protective man that he was. And who instead had hated him, setting him up for failure time and time again. Making him doubt himself and his kingship. Turning his caring nature against him so that he had to lie, so that he had to be someone he was never meant to be.

'You haven't failed, Galen,' she said thickly, emotion clogging her throat. 'I don't know what it will take for you to believe that, but you haven't. And you won't. It was you who were failed. Your father—'

'My father thought I wasn't his son, Solace.' His voice was bleak as midwinter. 'He saw nothing in me to make him change his mind, nothing that made him want to at least try to be a decent father.'

'That wasn't your fault. That was all him.'

'And what if it turns out that I am his son

after all?' His voice had become rougher. 'What if my own father just hated me? Because there's something...wrong in me.'

Pain welled up inside her. 'No. There is nothing—*nothing*—wrong with you.'

'How can you know that? There has to be a reason.'

She was aching to cross the distance between them, to put her hands on his broad chest and lean against him, soothe him, warm him, reassure him, but she didn't know if he would welcome it, so she stood where she was. 'I was never given a reason for Katherine to change her mind. And you told me she was wrong. You said, "Who wouldn't want you?"' She swallowed. 'So, I'm telling you now, I don't know why your father treated you the way he did, but he was wrong, Galen. He was *so* wrong. Because there's nothing wrong with you. You are the most special man I know. You're a wonderful father and an amazing king who feels so deeply about his country.' Something slipped down her cheek, a tear she hadn't quite managed to blink away. 'Those aren't failures. Those aren't mistakes. They're triumphs. And that's who you are. You're a triumph and you don't have to be anyone else.'

He looked at her for one long, aching minute. Then without a word he turned and walked out.

CHAPTER TEN

GALEN WAITED IN the small antechamber to the palace ballroom, listening to the music and buzz of conversations from the guests in the ballroom itself.

It was Solace's presentation ball and he'd kept the guest list to a minimum—a mere five hundred people. But he'd put all his effort into making sure this ball was the most magnificent the palace had ever put on, filling the room full of flowers and delicate lights and music. There was a fountain in the middle and serving staff circulating with the best champagne and the finest food. The atmosphere was one of joy and happiness and excitement, and, since he'd been practising his smile for the past week, he was sure no one would know how hollow he felt inside.

He hadn't seen Solace since that day at the house by the sea, where he'd confessed so many things he wished he hadn't, all those terrible doubts spilling out of him. He'd said too much.

And she'd only looked at him with that intense silver gaze and told him there was nothing wrong with him, told him everything he was... A triumph, she'd said.

But he didn't recognise that man. It wasn't him.

He'd had to leave in the end. He'd had to turn around and walk out of the door, because he couldn't bear it. He wanted so badly to be all the things she'd told him he was, but he never would and one day she'd see it too.

All week he'd been waiting for word that she'd changed her mind and left Kalithera, and half of him had debated cancelling the ball in preparation. But he hadn't heard a thing since he'd walked out on her, and so he had to assume that she still wanted the marriage to go ahead.

He couldn't imagine why, not after what he'd told her.

He looked down at his watch. She was a little late. What if today was the day she changed her mind? What if she left him standing here? He hadn't given her any reason to stay, and if she decided to take Leo and go back to London, well... He'd decided he wouldn't stop her. It would be no less than he deserved.

His fingers felt cold. Everything felt cold.

Abruptly the door opened, and his heart leapt, but when he turned from his contemplation of the empty fireplace it was to see Augustine stride in with Khalil close behind him.

Of course, he'd invited the pair of them, but they should be in the ballroom with the rest of the guests.

Galen told himself he wasn't disappointed and frowned as Khalil shut the door firmly. 'You two shouldn't be in here.'

Augustine shrugged. 'You know I'm always where I shouldn't be.'

'And I don't take orders,' Khalil added casually.

'Also...' Augustine strolled over to the fireplace where Galen stood '...where is the welcome, lovely to see you and thanks for coming?'

Galen stared coldly at them. 'You should be with the guests in the ballroom. I'm waiting here for my fiancée.'

'Ah yes,' Augustine murmured. 'The fiancée you neglected to tell us about.'

Khalil came up to stand on Galen's other side, giving him an enigmatic glance. 'You don't look like a man about to get married,' he observed.

'And what does that look like?' Acid had crept into his tone and he didn't wait for Khalil to reply. 'It's a royal marriage, what do you expect?' He glanced at Augustine. 'She's the daughter of a perfectly respectable—'

'She is not,' Khalil interrupted in his cool

way. 'Do not bother with the palace lies. We know the truth.'

'Indeed, we do,' Augustine agreed. 'Though it's exceptionally irritating to have to find out all of this ourselves since our supposed friend neglected to tell us.'

There was a stunned silence.

He hadn't told his friends, not the truth about Leo's origins and not about Solace. It had felt too complicated, and it led too close to his own secret, and both men were far too sharp to be fobbed off with the same lies. It was easier to not bring it up at all.

Galen turned to face the empty fireplace, putting his hands on the white marble mantelpiece and leaning against it. He said nothing. What could he say? If they knew everything?

'Why are you marrying her?' Augustine asked, his tone absolutely neutral.

'Because she had my child,' Galen bit out. 'And I need a wife. And she's—'

Fierce and brave and beautiful. Sharp and cool on the outside, but so soft and hot on the inside. Honest and determined and resourceful...

'I think you do not want to marry her,' Khalil said. 'I think you—'

'I'm marrying her,' Galen growled and shoved himself away from the mantelpiece, giving his friends a furious look. 'I promised her I would and so I am.'

'And you're obviously very happy about it,' Augustine observed. 'Congratulations?'

'It wasn't supposed to be about emotion,' Galen said, not even realising he'd been going to speak until it came out. 'It's a royal marriage. No feelings should be involved.'

'No,' Augustine murmured soothingly. 'Of course not.'

Khalil watched him with enigmatic dark eyes. 'Then why are you so angry about it?'

'Because she deserves more than I can give her,' he snapped. 'I promised her I'd marry her, and I don't want to break my word, but I'm condemning her to a loveless marriage and she needs more from me than that.'

Augustine and Khalil stared at him.

'But you do not love her,' Khalil said.

'No, but—'

'Why not?' Khalil tilted his head like a bird of prey, eyeing him. 'Is she somehow unlovable?'

'No, of course not.'

'Then I fail to see the problem.' Augustine waved a hand. 'Just…give her the love she deserves.'

'What? You think it happens on command? That it's that easy?'

'If you say she's worth it, then I don't see why not.'

It was clear neither of his friends knew what they were talking about, and Galen opened his mouth to tell them that, when the door opened again and this time it was Solace who came in.

He felt as if someone had hit him over the head.

She was dressed in the beautiful silver gown she'd worn the last time he'd seen her, only this time her hair had been pinned on top of her head in a soft bun, tendrils around her ears. A delicate platinum tiara set with diamonds glittered on her brow and around her throat was a matching diamond collar. There were small diamonds in her ears, and she glittered and sparkled as if she'd been set with stars.

She looked every inch a queen and she was here. She hadn't left. She was *here*.

'You're mad,' Augustine muttered. 'It is that easy. I'm in love with her already.'

'Indeed,' Khalil said, his voice getting deeper, a definite appreciation vibrating in the word.

Possessiveness turned over inside Galen. Solace was *his* queen, not theirs. 'Out,' he ordered. 'Now.'

Solace lifted a brow as the other two sauntered towards her.

Augustine paused beside her. 'Allow me to—'

'You can introduce yourself later,' Galen growled. 'Get out.'

His friends glanced at each other and, for some reason, both smiled. Then they left the room, closing the door firmly after them.

Solace came over to him and stopped. Then she lifted her hands and smoothed the black fabric of his jacket, making sure the decorations and awards pinned to the breast were lying flat. Then she fussed with the black bow tie he wore, touching him as if she had every right, as if he were hers already.

His chest ached and ached. It hadn't stopped aching since he'd left her a week earlier. He felt as if something inside him, a part of him, had broken beyond repair and now the jagged edges were grinding together, causing him agony.

'What are you doing?' His voice was rougher than it should have been.

'Making sure my fiancé is presentable.' She looked up at him, grey eyes shining. 'Did you think I wouldn't come?'

'I...' He couldn't finish. His voice refused to work, his fingers icy.

'Of course, I came,' she said, as if there had been no doubt whatsoever. 'But I'm not here for the crown, Galen. I'm here for you.'

'Solace, I can't—'

'I know,' she said simply. 'You were clear. There's something wrong with you. You don't want to fail me, and you don't know what love is, I get all of that.' She reached for his cold hands and gathered them in her small ones, her skin so warm against his. 'But like I told you last week, you haven't failed me, and you haven't failed Leo either. You haven't failed your country. And I can show you that there's nothing wrong with you. I can teach you. Perhaps it will take time, but I don't care. I have the time. Also, and most important, I know what love is.' She lifted his hands and brushed a light kiss over his knuckles. 'And I love you. Our marriage won't be loveless, Galen, because I can love enough for both of us.'

'Just give her the love she deserves,' Augustine had said. *'If you say she's worth it, then I don't see why not.'*

He stared down into her lovely face, into her grey eyes, and, as they had over a year ago, as they did every time he looked into them, they pierced his soul.

And it came to him like a revelation straight from God that if there was anyone in his life he trusted, it was her, and if he didn't trust her to teach him about love, if he didn't trust her vision of who he was, then his father had been right all along.

That all he was was an unfit king and a hated son.

Except Solace shouldn't have to teach him. Solace shouldn't have to love for both of them.

'There's nothing wrong with you,' she'd told him, before listing all the things that were right about him, all the good things. 'Your father was wrong.'

Why would you believe him when you have her?

He didn't know. But right now, with her small hands holding his, he knew if he didn't trust her vision of him, if he didn't trust her with everything in him, then that would be one mistake he'd regret for the rest of his life.

Because you love her.

He couldn't breathe, the moment drawing out, suspended for an eternity as he looked into her eyes, a feeling rushing through him, raw and powerful and relentless. Growing bigger and wider and deeper with every passing second. The sweetest, most welcome kind of agony.

But it wasn't new. He'd felt it before. He'd felt it the very instant he'd seen her in that ballroom fifteen months earlier. And it had been there all this time, waiting for him to recognise it for what it was. He'd given it so many names, lust, desire, need, obsession, yet none of them had felt right. None of them encompassed its true nature.

It was love. And he'd been running from it for far too long.

He was tired of running, just as he was tired

of all those other things he'd been doing for years now, and especially tired of the self-doubt his father had instilled in him over the years.

Because there was no self-doubt now, not about this. Not about her.

He loved her and he was never letting her go.

'No,' he said quietly. Then stronger. 'No.' And he adjusted their hands so hers were enclosed in his, his fingers no longer feeling quite so cold. 'You've done everything on your own for far too long and that ends here. It ends tonight.'

There was uncertainty in her eyes. 'What do you mean?'

She'd told him once he had to decide for himself who he was, and he knew now what that was supposed to be.

He was supposed to be her husband. He was supposed to love her.

'I don't know how it's supposed to feel,' he said roughly. 'But when I'm with you I can't think of anything else. When I'm with you all I want to do is touch you, kiss you. All I want to do is stay as close to you as possible and talk with you, listen to you laugh. Watch you smile. I want to know everything about you, every single thing, and I would kill anyone who hurt you. And I want to take care of you for the rest of your life and make sure you never know a moment's pain.'

Her eyes filled with sudden tears. 'Galen...'

He brought her hand to his mouth and kissed it, holding her shimmering gaze with his. 'And if that's love then I love you, Solace Ashworth. I have loved you since the moment I met you.'

Her hands were shaking. Everything was shaking. This was the last thing she'd expected.

She'd spent the past week half in tears, weeping over him, and half in a fury. A dozen times she'd packed a bag, determined to walk out and leave him, only to get to the front door and stop, because of course she wasn't going anywhere.

She couldn't walk away from him. He had no one. He was the world's loneliest king and if she left him, she knew she'd never forgive herself.

She was in it now, and of course she knew why.

She'd fallen in love with him body and soul.

Leaving him was impossible.

Which left her only one option. To stay and to show him exactly what love meant by loving him every day for the rest of their lives.

She could do it. She could be his queen. She could be his wife and live with him, and, in the end, she would show him.

Love had driven her from London to Kalithera, and love would keep her here, because love was her strength and it always had been.

So, she'd stayed and tonight had dressed with extra care, embracing that fire in her heart, and even though when she'd seen him standing by the cold fireplace, so impossibly beautiful in his evening clothes, the heavy gold signet ring of state on his finger, and yet, despite his friends, so alone, she'd nearly burst into tears.

But she wouldn't. She'd show him her strength. Show him that she wasn't going anywhere.

She'd expected to cry later, after the evening had ended, not now.

Except she couldn't help it, there were tears on her cheeks, ruining her make-up, and she couldn't stop them.

He loved her. He really did.

'Galen,' she said again, but he'd bent to kiss her now and his mouth was hot and sweet, the kiss telling her everything he hadn't said. That he was sorry, and he'd missed her, and he was so hungry for her he might die.

She leaned into him, feeling his warm arms wrap around her, holding her tight. 'Don't let me go,' she whispered against his mouth. 'Don't ever let me go. I love you, Galen Kouros, and I want to spend for ever with you. Promise me.'

'I promise,' he murmured. 'You're mine for ever, silver girl.'

Then, because they had duties to fulfil and

from now on there always would be, he pulled back and wiped away her tears, helped her fix her make-up, and then they went to the ballroom doors to be announced.

The evening went off without a hitch, and she was note-perfect with her story. Even Kostas couldn't find anything to be suspicious about.

Not that the majority cared. All they wanted to know was where she got her gown from and all they wanted to say was how beautiful she was, and lucky Galen to have caught her, and how in love they both seemed to be.

He didn't let her go all evening, not once.

It was the most magical night of Solace's life.

After it was over, even though it wasn't quite the done thing since they weren't married, Galen picked her up and carried her to the wing of the palace where his private rooms were and took her into his bedroom.

And right in the centre of the room was the biggest four-poster bed, piled high with pillows and hung with gauzy curtains.

A princess bed.

Solace had no words. She couldn't even speak.

But when he took her in his arms and carried her over to the bed, putting her down onto it, she pulled his mouth down on hers and showed him exactly how much it meant to her with all the passion in her soul.

And all the love in her heart.

They were married the following week, in a small, private ceremony, attended only by two kings and one very small boy.

And they lived happily ever after.

EPILOGUE

Twenty years later

GALEN SAT AT his desk in his office, staring at the email from the DNA company. He hadn't opened it yet and he didn't know if he wanted to. He didn't even know why he'd done the test, though, to be fair, he'd been thinking of his children and the legacy he would leave them. He didn't want them to feel the same uncertainty he had.

Then again, did it even matter after so many years? Kostas had passed away not long after he and Solace had married, taking the threat that had been hanging over Galen's throne with him. And Galen's four children were happy and healthy and thriving, so maybe it didn't.

At that moment, the door opened, and his wife came in, looking stunning in one of his favourite dresses, a simple white one with ties at the shoulders he could undo whenever he wanted to. Her hair was loose and there was a stormy expression on her face.

He loved it when she looked like that. It meant she wanted to argue about something, and he adored it when they argued. Especially when making up was so sweet.

'I have something to tell you,' she said, frowning.

'Oh? Wait, you're pregnant again?'

'No, of course not,' she said crossly. 'I'm way past that.'

He pushed back his chair and held out his arms imperiously.

She let out a little breath, jutted her chin a second, then finally came around the side of his desk and settled herself in her favourite place: his lap.

He put his arms around her, feeling her relax against him, the tension leaving her. 'Are you sure you're way past that?' he murmured.

She gave him a light swat then put her head on his chest and sighed. 'Don't get your hopes up.'

'My hopes are firmly centred on the conceiving part, it's true,' he admitted, settling her more comfortably against him. 'What is it you want to tell me?'

'You know, I can't even remember now.' She smiled and looked up at him. 'You still make me forget whatever it is that's bothering me almost immediately.'

He smiled back, the special smile he saved just for her. 'We don't have any immediate duties, do we?'

She always knew, because she seemed to know their schedules off by heart. She was a master organiser and a powerhouse when it came to getting things done, and as a queen she was formidable. She'd done much for the disadvantaged, especially children, and his subjects adored her.

Heat leapt in her eyes. The familiar heat that had always been between them and that still burned as brightly as it had years ago. 'No, I don't think so. And Xander is off trying to kill himself on that wretched skateboard of his.'

Xander was their youngest and the only one still at home. Leo was at Oxford—his choice—and doing extremely well studying mathematics. The twins Elena and Io were in the first year at university—Cambridge, so they didn't have to be near their brother—Elena studying physics and her sister medieval English literature.

Meanwhile, Xander, who wasn't at all academic but loved doing anything physical and especially loved it if it was dangerous, was busy turning his parents' hair white.

Galen loved them all to distraction, but he especially loved it when they were not around so he could do whatever he wanted to his beautiful wife.

'Excellent,' he murmured, then leaned forward and quickly deleted the email.

'What was that?' Solace asked.

'Nothing important,' he said, then he kissed her, and they both forgot about it.

Because that email didn't matter. It didn't matter who his father had been, or what his DNA was.

He knew who he was now. A king, a husband, a father, a lover.

With her, he'd found a home.

With her, he'd found a family.

With her, he'd found love.

With her, he'd found himself.

And there was nothing else he needed.

* * * * *

Did you fall head over heels for
Wed for Their Royal Heir?
*Then don't forget to look out for the next
instalment in the*
*Three Ruthless Kings trilogy
coming soon!*

*In the meantime
dive into these other magical stories
by Jackie Ashenden!*

Pregnant by the Wrong Prince
The Innocent's One-Night Proposal
A Diamond for My Forbidden Bride
Stolen for My Spanish Scandal
The Maid the Greek Married

Available now!